"You stay out here while I clear the place. I'm sure the burglar's long gone, but it doesn't hurt to be safe."

Danny couldn't help but watch as the man ran up the stairs. He had a superb ass. All of him was pretty superb, actually. Now that his panic was receding, Danny could actually appreciate the way the officer's slacks and button-down couldn't quite hide how nicely built he was. His face was attractive too.

And he was supernatural. He'd sniffed out that Danny was a werewolf immediately, but Danny couldn't place the officer's scent. He definitely wasn't a werewolf. He smelled earthy, like a shifter, but not anything Danny could pin down.

He heard the cop thundering down the stairs a few flights before he saw him, and he was ready when the man burst out of the door. He motioned Danny up the stairs.

Danny followed the detective inside.

WELCOME TO

DREAMSPUN BEYOND

Dear Reader,

Everyone knows love brings a touch of magic to your life. And the presence of paranormal thrills can make a romance that much more exciting. Dreamspun Beyond selections tell stories of love featuring your favorite shifters, vampires, wizards, and more falling in love amid paranormal twists. Stories that make your breath catch and your imagination soar.

In the pages of these imaginative love stories, readers can escape to a contemporary world flavored with a touch of the paranormal where love conquers all despite challenges, the thrill of a first kiss sweeps you away, and your heart pounds at the sight of the one you love. When you put it all together, you discover romance in its truest form, no matter what world you come from.

Love sees no difference.

Elizabeth North

Executive Director
Dreamspinner Press

Bru Baker

STEALING HIS HEART

WITHDRAWN

REAMSPUN BEYOND

PUBLISHED BY

REAMSPINNER
PRESS

Published by
DREAMSPINNER PRESS

5032 Capital Circle SW, Suite 2, PMB# 279,
Tallahassee, FL 32305-7886 USA
www.dreamspinnerpress.com

This is a work of fiction. Names, characters, places, and incidents either
are the product of author imagination or are used fictitiously, and any
resemblance to actual persons, living or dead, business establishments,
events, or locales is entirely coincidental.

Stealing His Heart
© 2019 Bru Baker.
Editorial Development by Sue Brown-Moore.

Cover Art
© 2019 Aaron Anderson.
aaronbydesign55@gmail.com
Cover content is for illustrative purposes only and any person depicted
on the cover is a model.

Paperback ISBN: 978-1-64108-152-8
Digital ISBN: 978-1-64405-198-6
Library of Congress Control Number: 2018961342
Paperback published March 2019
v. 1.0

Printed in the United States of America
∞
This paper meets the requirements of
ANSI/NISO Z39.48-1992 (Permanence of Paper).

BRU BAKER got her first taste of life as a writer at the tender age of four, when she started publishing a weekly newspaper for her family. What they called nosiness she called a nose for news, and no one was surprised when she ended up with degrees in journalism and political science and started a career in journalism.

Bru spend more than a decade writing for newspapers before making the jump to fiction. She now works in reference and readers' advisory in a Midwestern library, though she still finds it hard to believe someone's willing to pay her to talk about books all day. Most evenings you can find her curled up with a book or her laptop. Whether it's creating her own characters or getting caught up in someone else's, there's no denying that Bru is happiest when she's engrossed in a story. She and her husband have two children, which means a lot of her books get written from the sidelines of various sports practices.

Website: www.bru-baker.com
Blog: www.bru-baker.blogspot.com
Twitter: @bru_baker
Facebook: www.facebook.com/bru.baker79
Goodreads: www.goodreads.com/author/show/6608093.Bru_Baker
Email: bru@bru-baker.com

By Bru Baker

Published by **DREAMSPINNER PRESS**
www.dreamspinnerpress.com

For my family, both of blood and of choice, who help me make this dream of being a writer come true. You hold me up, and I am forever grateful. Rhys, C.S., Caraway, and Hunter, thanks for always being on the other end of the screen to talk me down from my more calamitous ideas.

Chapter One

DANNY hurried along the sidewalk, hugging his satchel close to his body to keep it dry. The torrential rain from earlier had eased, but he didn't want to take any chances with the remaining drizzle. It also made his satchel harder to steal, which was the real bonus.

He didn't live in the best of neighborhoods, but normally it didn't bother him. Most of the time he didn't have much to steal, but today he had a pair of iPads in his bag that probably cost more than the majority of the beater cars parked along the curb on his walk home.

He'd sold the Rolex his parents had given him for his high school graduation to buy these. Months of nonstop fundraising had paid for the rest of the bounty that was safely locked up in his apartment, but foster services had referred two more teens to the Janus Foundation last week, and he didn't want to leave them out of his gift-giving extravaganza.

His kids often came to their foster families with nothing, and Danny did whatever he could to ease their transitions and give them what they needed to succeed. This year he'd wanted to do something extra. Something special and completely impractical. The kids deserved a surprise, and he had a whopper planned for them.

Danny had grown up in a family that lacked for nothing. That Rolex would have been many people's prized possession, but he'd had two when he moved out of his parents' Manhattan townhome. He'd never worn either of them—he was more of a Casio guy at heart. Rough-and-tumble, waterproof, takes a lickin' and keeps on tickin'. No, wait. That was Timex.

He was living in what his father not-so-lovingly referred to as squalor. Danny poured all of his savings and the hefty inheritance he'd gotten when his grandmother died into the Janus Foundation. He drew enough of a salary to support himself, assuming he didn't splurge on things like a car. Or air-conditioning. Or that one notable month, dinner.

But it was worth it. When Jillian and Tomas, his newest charges at the day center, unwrapped these iPads, the gesture would mean a lot more to them than the Rolex had meant to him. The Janus Foundation served supernatural kids who had lost their parents, secretly working alongside the foster system to help support more than just their physical needs. The foster system was tough enough without worrying about how your foster family would react if you sprouted fur or accidentally broke a bookshelf with telekinesis.

So Danny provided a safe space for the kids to gather and hang out, in addition to helping pay for basics like clothes and school supplies since supernatural kids tended to be a bit harder on their possessions and DCFS would only buy a kid so many pairs of jeans before caseworkers started asking questions. He also made sure the kids had access to the things they needed to help keep them balanced, like regular trips to the river for nymphs and weekend campouts for druids and dryads who needed to reconnect to the earth.

Danny had been twenty-two when his parents verbally disowned him, and that had been hard. He couldn't even imagine the strength it took for these kids to keep soldiering on, day after day, when they couldn't be with their own kind.

Danny curled in on himself with a shout as a black town car passed too close, showering him with dirty water. He shifted his satchel away from the wetness, cursing the driver for cutting the corner.

He was almost home anyway. His only plans for the evening involved Netflix and sitting in front of the fan in his boxers.

He'd wrap the iPads and add them to the stash in his coat closet, and then his responsibilities for the Janus Foundation would be done until the big back-to-school party in three weeks. He couldn't wait to hand out the presents. He'd picked something expressly for each kid, whether it was an iPad or a laptop or expensive software or accessories, and he couldn't wait to see their faces. Each present was tailored to their interests. It wasn't really the cost that would make it so special—it was the thought that went into it and the extravagance of the gesture. Who buys a foster kid a GoPro? One of the few adults in her life who knew she wanted to be a filmmaker and had been secretly making documentaries with her crappy borrowed Motorola phone, that's who.

He had plans for music and lots of food and expected the gift giving to be absolute chaos. He couldn't wait.

Danny jogged up the two steps to his building's foyer, muttering lowly when the security door opened with the slightest touch. It was supposed to be locked all the time, but it hardly ever was. He didn't even try the elevator, which was out of service more than it was in, and trudged up the three flights of poorly lit stairs to his floor.

Half of the apartments were either vacant or had bright orange eviction notices taped to them. It made his heart hurt to think of the Robinsons, a nice family of four who'd lived next door until a few days ago. He'd helped out whenever he could, leaving them bags of groceries and helping the kids with their homework when they were home alone after school, but they'd needed more assistance than he could give them.

His father said his willingness to bend over backward for strangers was his biggest character flaw. It was ironic that a person who gave away millions every year for a photo op would turn his nose up at giving a family in need a bag full of canned goods.

Then again, his father had probably never *seen* a bag full of canned goods. God knows Danny had been surprised you could get things like meat in a can when he'd struck out on his own.

Danny's heart jumped into his throat when he realized his apartment door was ajar. He'd definitely locked and dead bolted it this morning when he'd left for work. He pushed the door open, swallowing hard when it fell off its hinges in a cloud of dust and splintered wood.

Break-ins weren't that common around here, mostly because no one had anything worth stealing. Hell, he didn't even have a TV. But he did have a closet full of almost fifteen grand in gifts.

Danny rushed into his apartment, wincing at the way the door whined and cracked under his weight. His living room looked exactly like it had when he'd left, right down to the cereal bowl on the coffee table. The only thing amiss was the coat-closet door, which was wide open and revealed a few scarves on the ground and the pair of boots with the floppy sole he kept meaning to have repaired.

"Oh fuck." Horror welled in his throat, making it hard to swallow.

They were gone.

His stomach lurched and he had to blink quickly to stem the hot flood of tears that threatened. He was not going to cry or throw up or sit down and bury his head in his knees.

He was an adult, dammit, and he could deal with this on his own.

Danny stared at the empty closet.

He could *not* deal with this on his own.

"Siri, call Sloane."

His cousin was in her last year of med school. She was several years younger, but she'd been his designated adult since his parents had all but written him off when he'd pursued a master's degree in social work.

She didn't pick up, so he called again.

His knees almost buckled in relief when she answered this time. Sloane would know what to do. She'd tell him how to fix this.

"Danny, it's not a good ti—"

"My place got robbed, and everything is gone," he said in a rush, his voice wobbling. So much for handling this like an adult.

"Fuck. Hold on a sec, okay? I have to leave class so I can talk."

He'd forgotten she was still on campus. Shit.

"I'm back. What the hell happened? Are you okay? Were you there? What did the police say?"

Danny blinked at his splintered door. "I haven't talked to the police yet. I just got home."

"Oh my God!"

Danny had to hold the phone away from his ear, cringing as she shrieked.

"Get out of your apartment, you idiot! What if they're still there?"

Fuck, he hadn't thought of that. He tamped down the panic building in his chest. "I'm a werewolf, Sloane. What is a burglar going to do to me?"

"I don't know, *shoot you*?" she said, voice dripping with sarcasm.

A bullet wouldn't kill him, not unless it was a head shot, but it wouldn't feel good either. And to be honest, he was a bit wimpy when it came to werewolf powers. He'd grown up in Manhattan, for Christ's sake. It wasn't like he was a tough guy. Besides, Alpha Connoll would have his balls if he shifted in front of a human.

"Right," Danny said, glancing behind himself as he gingerly stepped over the door. "Okay, I'm in the hallway."

Sloane sighed. "Outside, Danny. Go outside. Wait for the police to come."

Danny wrapped an arm around his satchel, pressing the weight of the two boxes inside it against his side as he ran down the steps. He sure as hell wasn't going to lose these. If the burglar was still around, he'd have to peel them out of Danny's cold, dead claws.

Was that sexist, to assume a burglar was a man? It could have been a lady burglar. Or that would probably just be *burglar*, right? Putting lady in front of something was definitely sexist.

"Are you outside?"

Danny nearly dropped the phone he still held pressed to his ear. He'd forgotten about Sloane.

"What if it's a woman?"

"What if *what* is a woman? Are you outside or not, Danny? Jesus."

"Yes, I'm out front. What if the burglar is a woman?"

"Oh my God, you're losing it. Listen, I'm hanging up. Call the police, and I'll be there as soon as class is over."

Danny probably *was* losing it. The burglar's gender didn't matter here. It was just his brain trying to distract him from the growing panic in his chest. He'd used tangents like that to help control his shift right after his Turn, and old habits apparently died hard.

"Police," he muttered to himself. "Right."

He dialed 911, looking around nervously. That number was for big stuff. Should he be calling the nonemergency…?

"911, what's your emergency?"

Danny nearly fumbled the phone in his sweaty palm. "Um, I need to report a burglary?"

Damn it. It sounded like he was questioning whether or not there had been one. He needed to pull himself together.

"I mean, my apartment has been robbed, and I need to report it."

"Is the burglar still on the premises?"

"I don't know? I could go in and check—"

"No, sir. If you're outside, please stay there until an officer arrives. Can you give me your address?"

Danny ran through all the information with her, and she assured him a uniformed officer would come by to clear his apartment and take his statement. Then she disconnected.

Weren't 911 operators supposed to stay on the line with you until help arrived? Or maybe that was only in case of a life-threatening emergency.

Danny sat on the steps and put his bag in his lap, curling around it protectively. The rain had let up, at least. The operator'd told him to stay where he was, but if it started up again he'd have to move inside, where Mr. Rodriguez in 1A would yell at him for blocking the mailboxes.

He held off looking at his watch for what seemed like an hour, only to discover it had barely been fifteen minutes. Was it normal to take this long for police to respond? What if the burglar was still in his apartment? They'd have gotten away by now.

What if the burglar came out this way? The back way out took a winding path through the laundry room and the building's basement. It wasn't marked, so if the burglar didn't know the building, he probably wouldn't be able to find it. That meant the burglar would be coming this way, right past Danny on the front steps.

Shit.

Danny cursed at himself for not taking better note of his surroundings when he'd been upstairs. What kind of werewolf panicked so hard in the face of danger that he didn't even think to listen for heartbeats in the room? He could have solved the question of whether or not the thief was still there in ten seconds.

God, he couldn't even remember what the apartment smelled like. Everyone left a scent trail, and that closet had been full—it wouldn't have been a quick job to load it all up and haul it out. There should have been a trail he could follow to see if the thief had left the building.

Danny hesitated. He could go back in and check, but he'd promised Sloane he'd stay outside. And what would he do if someone *was* still in the apartment? Jump him? He didn't trust himself not to wolf out under the pressure, and that would make this an even bigger clusterfuck.

He checked his watch. Twenty minutes.

If the police still hadn't come by the time Sloane showed up, they'd go in together. They could take a human burglar together, no problem. And having her there would ground him and he wouldn't shift. Probably.

She certainly wouldn't. His cousin had great control. She'd only had to stay one month at Camp H.O.W.L., but it had taken Danny two months to get his shit together enough not to sprout fur and fangs when he got startled. Hell, it was still a struggle. There was a reason his father referred to their wolf side as the beast.

Maybe that's why he identified so hard with the kids he worked with. He knew what it felt like to have everything on the line and worry constantly that he'd be the one to out the supernatural world to humans.

Fuck. Those kids meant everything to him, and thinking about how much he'd let them down by not storing their presents somewhere safer made his stomach hurt. They didn't even know they were getting them—he threw a back-to-school party every year and gave them basic school supplies, so that's what they assumed this party would be. They were so damn grateful for backpacks and pencils. He'd really wanted to do something special for them. Show them that they were loved.

It had been forty minutes by the time an unmarked police car with lights on the dash pulled up. He wouldn't have noticed it if he wasn't watching for it. It slid into a space across the street, and Danny shot up, waving his hand frantically so the officers could see him. Only one guy got out, and he wasn't wearing a uniform. When he turned and started walking down the street, Danny streaked after him, using more speed than was cautious. He dodged a Prius. Its driver slammed on the brakes and honked, and the cop turned around. He stopped and watched Danny run, and

Danny didn't slow down until he noticed the calculated way the guy was looking at him.

This was why he rarely used his Were strength or senses. He was so bad at hiding it.

"You got a problem, buddy?" the cop asked when Danny skidded to a stop in front of him. "Pretty dangerous move you just pulled there."

When the cop squinted at him, Danny remembered a human would be out of breath after a stunt like that. He heaved his chest as best he could, but the cop just rolled his eyes and took him by the arm, pulling him into an alley between buildings.

"Look, you can cut it out. I can smell you're a wolf. What the hell are you trying to pull?"

Danny's fake hyperventilation turned into an actual gasp, which triggered a coughing fit. He hunched over, and the cop smacked him on the back a few times, hard enough to bruise a human.

"My apartment was robbed, but you were heading the wrong way. I wanted to catch you before I had to wait another forty minutes for someone else to show up."

The guy gave him a long look. "You called dispatch?"

"They said they were sending someone right out."

The cop laughed. "You could be waiting a lot longer."

Danny couldn't help the way his lower lip trembled. He swallowed hard, but he knew the cop had scented his tears. The guy's nostrils flared, and his face softened.

"I'm coming off shift. I'll come over and take a report. You live across the street?" he nodded toward Danny's building. Mr. Rodriguez had come out, probably drawn by the screech of brakes and honking. He had his arms crossed, and he was looking right at Danny.

"Let me call it in and tell dispatch I'm taking it," the guy said.

He walked back to the car, got in, and fiddled with the radio. Danny tuned it out, not wanting to hear how he might recount the story. It had been stupid to run blindly across the street like that. He'd just been so worried when the guy went the wrong way.

After he finished with the radio, the guy got out and popped his trunk. His movements were sure and economical as he opened a safe and took out a scary looking black gun, which he strapped to his waist.

"What unit?" he asked as he slammed the trunk shut.

Danny gave him directions to his apartment, and the two of them crossed the street at a much more sedate pace than Danny's first crossing. Mr. Rodriguez had disappeared by the time they reached the steps, which was the first thing that had gone Danny's way all afternoon.

"You stay out here while I clear the place. I'm sure the burglar's long gone, but it doesn't hurt to be safe."

Danny couldn't help but watch as the man ran up the stairs. He had a superb ass. All of him was pretty superb, actually. Now that his panic was receding, Danny could actually appreciate the way the officer's slacks and button-down couldn't quite hide how nicely built he was. His face was attractive too.

And he was supernatural. He'd sniffed out that Danny was a werewolf immediately, but Danny couldn't place the officer's scent. He definitely wasn't a werewolf, and he wasn't fae either. He smelled earthy, like a shifter, but not anything Danny could pin down.

He'd had a gun. Did that mean he shifted into something that didn't have claws? Though as a cop he wouldn't be able to use them, so that's probably why he had the gun.

He heard the cop thundering down the stairs a few flights before he saw him, and he was ready when the man burst out of the door. He had stowed his gun, and he didn't look nervous or upset. He motioned Danny up the stairs.

Danny followed the detective inside.

"No one was in your apartment, but it doesn't hurt to make sure," he told Danny over his shoulder. "You had a pretty flimsy lock on that door. It wouldn't have taken much to break it."

The detective had moved the door aside instead of walking over it like Danny had. It was in pieces, and he had no idea what he was going to do about it. His super was useless, so Danny would have to figure out how to salvage the door until he could get someone to come by and put up a new one. God only knew how much that was going to cost him.

"It doesn't look like they tossed the place. Do you know what's missing?"

The lump in Danny's throat grew. "A lot. I'm the director of the Janus Foundation, and I was storing things for the foundation here. We'd raised enough money to give each of the kids we work with a laptop or an iPad for the start of school."

The detective winced. "How many kids does your foundation serve?"

"About forty," Danny said. He hesitated, then looked up at the detective. "They're all Supes. I have a network of social workers who refer kids. On paper the foundation serves hard-to-place kids in the foster system. Someday I hope we can fund a facility so these kids don't have to go into the regular foster system, but I don't have that kind of fundraising power right now. But social workers know when a kid is different, you know? And they refer them to me. Not all of the referrals are actually Supes, and those kids I refer on to other agencies that can help. But a good number of them are supernatural kids, and I work to get them placed with families that can handle them and get them the resources they need. Money for nymphs and dryads to go to summer camp up in Maine, grants for selkies and shifters to attend smaller private schools where their senses won't get overwhelmed, or funds to retrofit a foster family's house with insulated wiring so witchlings and mages can't short-circuit it—that kind of stuff."

The detective looked stunned. "I had no idea. I mean, in my Pack, no kid would ever be left to the foster system. I can't even imagine it."

Danny grimaced. "It's totally against our instincts to let one of our Pack fend for themselves, but not all Supes belong to a functional Pack. Some of them get tossed out because a new Alpha takes over and the kid is a threat. With witchlings and mages, sometimes they're surfacing after years of the bloodline being dormant, and parents don't understand what's going on. They think the kid is just trouble."

He'd never had a werewolf, but that was probably just because Weres didn't actually go through the Turn and gain their supernatural abilities until the first full moon after their nineteenth birthday. Most shifters and other supernatural beings had their powers from birth. He couldn't fathom what growing up that way would be like—he'd presented as 100 percent human until his Turn. All Were kids did. Scientists didn't know why Weres were different, but he suspected it was some sort of biological coping mechanism. Weres were more common nowadays, probably because they'd developed the second puberty as a means to hide among humans.

"I can't believe I didn't know about this." The cop shook his head. "I mean, we've got a network of Supes on the force. We should be keeping an eye out for kids who need help."

Maybe this was the silver lining to this incredibly shitty day. Danny had a few ins with the police since two of his Pack members were officers, but maybe this guy could expand that.

"If you're serious about helping, we can set up a time to meet and talk about it. I'm always looking for new contacts."

"What are you going to do about the stuff that was stolen? Are you insured?"

Danny winced. "No, not for something like that."

"Shit," the detective muttered. He dug out his wallet and shoved a wad of cash at Danny. "It's not much, but it's a start. I'll talk to my Pack about getting a donation together. Maybe you can raise enough money to replace the stolen stuff."

Danny felt awkward taking the money, but he shoved it in his pocket anyway. He wasn't in the position to turn any help down.

"I really appreciate that. Thank you. Is there any chance of getting my stuff back, do you think?"

"Honestly? No. They're long gone by now, and even if you found them in pawn shops there wouldn't be a way to prove they were yours, not unless you have all the serial numbers."

Which he definitely didn't. He hadn't unwrapped any of them. He'd wanted the kids to know they were brand-new and not refurbished hand-me-downs. He was kicking himself for it now.

"If you send me a list of everything that was stolen, I can get it in the official report, but it's not going to do you much good. Even though this was a huge blow for you, it's not really big enough for us to investigate. Not unless you have an idea of who might have done this. Who knew you were keeping them here?"

"No one except my cousin Sloane, and she's one of the donors."

That wasn't exactly true, Danny realized. Joss, one of the older kids who was a regular at the day center, knew about them. He'd been there when Danny had signed for a big delivery, and he knew where Danny lived because he'd been the Janus Foundation's first client, way back when Danny had been working out of this apartment, before the lease on the office was finalized. But Joss would never do something like this. Would he?

"Do you have a plan for securing that door?"

Danny followed the detective's gaze over to the open space where his door used to be.

"No," he admitted. Maybe he could use duct tape to put the door pieces back together? He could prop it up with a couple kitchen chairs.

The detective sighed and ran a hand through his hair. "Okay, here's what we're going to do. I'll file what I got from you and hand it off to the officers who should have taken your statement in the first place. And then I'm going to call one of my brothers, and we'll fix your door."

Danny gaped at him. "You don't have to—"

The detective cut him off with a sharp look. "I'm not going to leave you with an unsecured door in a neighborhood like this. And I'm not doing it as a cop. I'm doing it as a neighbor."

He held his hand out, and Danny took it. It was warm and soft, and the brief contact of their handshake was more comforting than Danny wanted to admit.

"I'm Max, and I live across the street. It's great to meet you. I'll be back in about an hour to help with your door."

Chapter Two

"LOOK, can you come or not? I need an extra set of hands to get this door fixed, and the guy doesn't look like he'd know which end of a hammer is which. He'd probably end up breaking it even more."

Max should have asked one of his neighbors instead of calling Ray. All of his brothers were assholes, and Ray was no exception. But he was the closest and most likely to drop everything and come, which is why Max chose him.

"Oh, I'll be there. I haven't heard you this hot and bothered by a guy in a long time."

Max's face heated. "It's not like that. He's just some clueless kid who needs help. What was I supposed to do, let him live in that pit without a functioning door? The rest of his stuff would be stolen by morning."

Danny wasn't a kid. Max had pulled his driver's license when he filed the police report. Danny was two years younger than him, though with his baby face he looked more like twenty-two than thirty-two. Besides, he wasn't Max's type at all. His last boyfriend had been a CrossFit instructor, and the one before that was one of the firefighters from Ray's station. Max didn't go for boyishly handsome, slender guys like Danny. Not even ones who smelled irresistible.

"How many burglary reports did you take before your hotshot promotion, hmm? And you stayed to fix all those doors too, right?"

He had a point. Normally Max could close the figurative door on a case and walk away when his job was finished, but there was something different about this one. Maybe it was how clueless Danny was, or how upset he'd been.

"He's a Were," Max said. "The Supe community should stick together."

Ray hummed noncommittally, and Max caved.

"Okay, fine. Yes. He's hot. And he needed my help, and I couldn't just leave him there."

He held the phone away from his ear as Ray whooped and hollered.

"So are you coming?"

Max rooted around in his toolbox, cursing under his breath. He didn't have enough screws for what he was planning.

"Hell yes, I'm coming."

"Can you stop by the hardware store on your block? His door is in pieces, and I don't have enough wood screws. Might need some plywood to reinforce it too."

"I'll see what I can do. His building's going to replace it, right? This is just to get him through the night?"

Max had looked at that place when he'd been apartment hunting. It was in horrible shape, and there were several complaints on file with the housing board about the super refusing to fix things.

"Probably not," Max said. "He seemed to think replacing it was his responsibility."

"Gotcha," Ray said. Keys jingled on the other end of the line. "On my way. Gimme thirty, maybe forty, and I'll be there. Should I come to you or go right to his place?"

"There. I'm heading over in a few. I'll help him clean up, and we'll see if the door is salvageable."

He gave Ray the address and ignored the way his brother teased him about his impatience to get back to Danny.

Max rubbed at his chest, trying to chase away the unease that had settled there. Danny was a werewolf— he could take care of himself if need be. But something was pulling him back across the street.

He gave in and grabbed his toolbox. Logically he knew Danny was fine, but his instincts were going crazy. He wanted to be there to protect him even though he knew there wasn't any danger.

Danny was sitting in the hallway outside his apartment when Max made his way back over, and the sight of him put Max on instant alert.

"Something happen?"

Danny looked up at him and shook his head. "No, it was just depressing being in there. And since I don't have a door, I can't leave, so the hallway was my only option."

Max walked past him into the apartment. "I'll start getting cleaned up in here. My brother Ray will be here in a bit, and he's going to help me with the door."

Danny trailed behind him and took a seat on a rickety chair at the table. "I really appreciate your help, Max."

"I couldn't let you stay here without a door," he said, aware how silly that sounded. He didn't even know Danny. "Besides, it's not a big deal."

"It is a big deal," Danny said. His voice wavered, and he drew in on himself a bit. Max didn't like the way it made him look small. "I don't know anyone who'd be able to do this. I'd have to call a handyman or something and…. I-I'll pay you for the supplies, of course. And dinner's on me tonight."

Max glanced around. He'd gotten a vague impression of the place earlier when he'd cleared it, but now his gaze was drawn to the threadbare sofa and the kitchen table with duct tape on one of the metal legs. The walls were bare, and there were only a few knickknacks spread throughout the room. A single plate and cup sat in the dish drainer next to the chipped enamel sink, but aside from that there wasn't much evidence that anyone lived here. He didn't get the feeling a handyman would be an easy expense for Danny to swallow. Hell, he didn't even look like he could afford to feed two shifters for dinner. Max would have to find a way to pay for it without insulting him.

"Don't thank me till we get it fixed," he said, casting a sour look at the pieces of the door. "I'm not sure it'll hold with what I've got planned."

"Even if it's flimsy, it gives me time to bug the super. He'd fix it eventually."

Max heard the lie but didn't press Danny on it. He played basketball with a few werewolves, and he knew that rule was the same in Were and shifter culture. Keep your ears and nose to yourself.

He hated the thought of Danny here without a solid door. Hell, the thing was hollow—it had probably taken one good kick to shatter it. He needed something a lot sturdier living in a place like this.

Max's place across the street wasn't much bigger, but it was in a lot better shape. He bet his rent was almost double too. At least he hoped Danny wasn't paying anything close to what Max paid a month. He certainly wasn't getting his money's worth if he did.

Ray called for him from five floors down, his tone low. Danny's head snapped up too, and his brows furrowed.

"That's my brother," Max explained. "He's the youngest, and we dropped him on his head a lot. It explains the lack of manners."

Ray said something unflattering about Max, and Danny burst out laughing. "He's very creative."

Max mumbled about younger siblings as he and Danny hurried downstairs.

"I'm an only child," Danny said softly. "I used to wish for a brother. My parents were too busy for one kid, let alone two. My cousin Sloane used to spend summers with us, and it was my favorite time of the year, having someone to hang out with. She's five years younger than me, but she was the closest thing I had to a sibling so I never minded having her around."

Max couldn't imagine being an only child. "I have three brothers and two sisters. Some solitude would have been nice."

"Solitude wouldn't have stopped and gotten you a door, asshole," Ray yelled from the street.

Max and Danny exchanged a look and hurried down the last flight of stairs. Danny's nosy neighbor was standing at the door yelling at Ray for loitering, but he stopped when he saw Max.

"You're the cop from earlier, right? I caught this one casing the place."

Ray's brows drew together. "You think I'm casing the place holding a gigantic door? Wouldn't that make me a little conspicuous?"

The man scowled at him.

"I'm so sorry about him," Danny cut in. He looked like he wanted the ground to swallow him. "Mr. Rodriguez, he's here to help me. My door was kicked in by the burglar."

That only seemed to confirm to the old man that they were up to no good. He wagged a finger in Danny's face.

"Don't think I won't tell the super about this," he muttered.

"Hey, how about you tell him one of his tenants had a break-in and fixed the door himself instead of waiting for the deadbeat super to fix it?"

The man scowled at Ray, who had poked his head around the door to snark at him.

"Damn drug dealers," the old man muttered as he slammed his door.

"I'll deal you a drug, you crotchety old bastard," Ray muttered as he moved his grip on the door so he could walk into the entryway with it. "Your other neighbors that nice, kid?"

"He's the same age as you, *kid*," Max snapped.

Danny's eyes widened at his tone, which made Max's cheeks heat in embarrassment. *Way to play it cool, Torres.* Ray was already two flights up, cackling to himself, but luckily Danny hadn't picked up on the taunt. Max would bet everything he owned that by the time he and Danny made it upstairs, Ray would have already texted the entire family that Max's latest love interest was only one step from the cradle.

Not that Danny was a love interest. He was just a guy who needed help.

Ray was leaning against the wall, shoving his phone back into his pocket when they made it back up. Dammit.

"It was so nice of you to come," Danny said. He held his hand out, and Ray gave Max an incredulous look before taking it. "Please let me know how much I owe you for the door."

Ray shrugged it off. "Don't worry about it. A guy owed me a favor."

Max opened the toolbox he'd brought over and started in on the hinges. Hopefully the door would fit. It had a solid wood core, so if it didn't, he and Ray could trim it down.

"You look really at home with that in your hands," Danny said, crouching down beside him.

Max's instincts preened, and he slapped the reaction down. He wasn't going to take advantage of the guy's gratitude.

"Our dad's a contractor," Ray answered. "We've been doing this shit since we were old enough to hold a screwdriver."

"Really? Wow. So you guys worked when you were kids?"

What the hell kind of Pack did Danny come from that he *didn't* get put to work as a kid? Max knew werewolves were different, since they didn't come into any of their powers until they were nineteen, but they still had a hierarchical Pack structure. Being a cub meant being the lowest rung on the ladder—he'd spent his childhood fetching things for older cousins and doing chores for his aunties and uncles. It was how things were done.

"Yeah, Pop brought us to job sites when he could."

Max snorted. "Go ahead and pretend you didn't grow up like a spoiled princess because you were the youngest, Ray-Ray."

"Fuck you, old man," Ray muttered, dropping the screws from the hinge he was working on so they fell in Max's hair.

Max looked over at Danny, whose gaze was darting between the two of them. Right. He hadn't had any siblings growing up. It probably looked like Max and Ray hated each other.

"If you think this is bad, you should see a family dinner," he said, grinning when Danny's eyes widened. "You'd think the guys would be the worst, but my sisters will draw actual blood if you piss them off."

"Ma's even scarier," Ray said. "Remember that time Phil and Theo broke the dining room table wrestling while they were shifted?"

Max shuddered at the memory. "What he neglects to mention is it was Thanksgiving, the table was full of food, and Ma has a strict no shifting in the house policy."

Danny whistled. "Bet they got grounded for life."

Ray started laughing so hard he had to stop what he was doing, and Max let out a few belly laughs himself. "It was three years ago. They didn't get grounded, but it might have been easier if they had. Their wives were not amused, especially when Ma said she wasn't going to host Thanksgiving anymore. We've been trading it around ever since."

"It's Max's turn this year. We all can't wait to see what kind of takeout he orders," Ray said with a snicker.

"Like I could afford enough takeout to feed the Pack," Max scoffed. "You guys eat like pigs."

"Gonna find yourself a nice man who can cook in the next four months?"

Danny shot him a hooded look that went straight to Max's groin. Max wondered if Danny knew how to cook.

"Maybe I'm going to take classes," Max said, winking at Danny. He flushed and looked away, which was interesting. "Maybe I'm a strong, independent shifter who doesn't need a man."

Ray laughed. "Okay, Beyoncé. Just give me a heads-up if you're cooking. I'll take the next day off at the station so I can deal with the food poisoning."

The last hinge hit the floor with a thunk, and Ray and Max stepped back to survey the opening.

"Frame's intact," Ray said, running a hand around it. "As long as the hinge placement matches up we're home free."

Max groaned and rubbed his palm against his face.

"He jinxed us," he explained when Danny raised an eyebrow at him.

"Shut up, I did not." Ray slapped Max across the back of the head. "Get over here and help me line up the door."

Ray hadn't jinxed them after all, and the two of them made short work of getting the new door installed. He left Ray to refit the old doorknob and add the shiny new dead bolt he'd brought over with the door, because even though he could be a bonehead sometimes, his brother was pretty damn thoughtful.

"Let's finish sweeping up all the debris now that the door is in," Max said, ignoring the raised eyebrow his brother gave him when he cupped Danny's elbow to lead him inside. He ignored the kissy faces Ray made, kicking him hard when he passed him.

"I can't believe it took you guys like twenty minutes to fix the door."

Max laughed. "We've got a lot of experience. Our parents are big believers in natural consequences. In a house full of shifter kids, that means fixing a lot of doors. One of the main reasons I went to work with Pop was to make enough money to replace the things I broke around the house."

Danny's smile lit up his face, which only highlighted the tired circles under his eyes. This guy needed about a week of sleep and someone to feed him. Max really wanted to be that someone, and it kind of freaked him out.

"I never had to deal with that. I can't imagine growing up with the ability to go wolf and the super strength and senses."

Max handed him the dustpan and started sweeping up the splintered wood and flakes of paint.

"Eh, we don't think much of it. It's just the way it is, you know? Most shifters are homeschooled until their control is solid, and some are homeschooled all the way through. In my Pack, we're homeschooled until high school. My sisters hated that. Girls usually have control way earlier than boys."

Danny scrunched up his face. "That must have been awful. Being homeschooled, I mean. Being stuck at home with my parents 24/7 would have been a nightmare."

Max was surprised by the vehemence behind Danny's words. It made him itch to find out more about Danny's childhood.

"It wasn't terrible. Besides, the parents in the Pack shared responsibilities, so it was more like having a weird multiage classroom. It wasn't always Ma."

It had been pretty great, actually. He remembered weekend campouts in the woods north of the city, full of laughter and running and the occasional botany lesson to make it educational.

"The happiest day of my life was when I left for boarding school when I was eleven," Danny said. "I was in private school before that. My parents were hardly ever home. I was raised by nannies until I was six, and then they deemed me old enough to stay with only the housekeeper. I never had a real sense of family until Sloane started spending summers with us."

That sounded terrible. And unnatural for a family of werewolves. Most Alphas worth their salt wouldn't allow a child to suffer like that.

"Is your family local?"

"Manhattan. My mother nearly fainted when I told her I was moving out here. I started the foundation with money I inherited from my grandmother, and my father strenuously objected. I see them at holidays and our monthly Pack events."

That would put them in Alpha Connoll's territory, which didn't make any sense. He was an upstanding guy and a great Alpha. Max had nothing but respect for the operation Alpha Connoll ran, and he couldn't imagine him standing for a wolfling being treated so coldly.

Then again, he had upward of 250 Weres in his pack. Maybe he just hadn't noticed.

Max swept a pile of debris into Danny's dustpan. He had a hard time believing someone like Danny could have flown under the radar—he wore his heart on his sleeve. Max had known him a couple of hours, and even he could see how much the guy was hurting and how lonely he was. Surely an Alpha would pick up on that immediately.

He sniffed discreetly, frowning when he couldn't smell anyone on Danny but himself. That meant he'd gone too long without scent marking or some sort of contact. There should have been strong scents surrounding him that Max's casual touches couldn't have erased so easily.

"Do you run with your Pack at the full moon, Danny?" he asked softly.

Danny frowned. "Of course I do."

The last moon had been a week ago. Danny should be thick with the scent of his Pack, but he didn't carry a single one of their scents.

"I had to miss the run last month because it was the only time a potential donor could meet, but I went for the Pack meal in the morning," Danny said defensively when Max didn't respond.

Hell. This guy was starving in more ways than one. He needed regular contact with his Pack as much as he needed food, and it didn't look like he was getting enough of either.

The sound of someone thundering up the stairs made both their heads snap up, but Max stood down when Danny's face opened up. He followed Danny out into the hall, staying behind as a blonde whirlwind tackled Danny.

"I got here as soon as I could. How are you? Do you need anything? What can I do to help? Do you need to come back to the house tonight?"

Danny laughed and untangled himself. "Take a breath, Sloane. I'm fine. Upset about the loss, but fine. Come meet the guys who are fixing my door."

He dragged her up, and Max ran his gaze over her, assessing the girl he assumed was Danny's cousin. She was tall, almost as tall as Danny, and they had the same nose, but that's where the similarities ended. She was slender but not as thin as Danny, who was gaunt where she was tanned and healthy. She flashed Max a million-watt smile, and his stomach soured as he took in her designer clothes and a haircut that probably set her back a few hundred a month. Family was supposed to help each other out. Why wasn't she making sure Danny had food and a decent place to live? It looked like she could afford it.

"Max, Ray, this is my cousin Sloane. Sloane, this is Max, the police officer who helped me out today. And Ray is his brother. He brought me a new door."

Sloane's eyes widened as she picked up on the scents in the room. "You've got people over. You never have people over."

Danny's embarrassment tickled at Max's nose. He tried to tune it out, letting Danny and Sloane have their whispered discussion while he helped Ray test the dead bolt. It slid home just fine, and the lock on the old doorknob still worked. He gave it a jiggle, satisfied when it stuck firmly in place.

He unlocked the door and stepped into the hallway, pretending he couldn't hear the argument Sloane and Danny were having in the living room.

The smell of his sister Tori's pork-belly pancit filled the stairwell, and he jabbed Ray in the ribs. That and the smell of adobo chicken drowned out the other scents in the air, but he could hear three heartbeats.

"Who did you call?" he asked Ray, poking a finger into his chest. "I told you I only wanted you."

"Aww, as touching as that is, did you really think I was going to keep this to myself? You never wig out over guys, and now you're panicking that some guy you just freaking met, who is a werewolf and can take care of himself, I might add, has a broken door? Bro, I called everyone."

Fucking hell.

"You told Ma?" Max whispered harshly.

"What? No! Of course not. I don't have a death wish. I sent out a message on our group chat."

Max and his siblings were all on the same group chat, which they mostly used to bitch about their parents and razz on each other. There was a separate family chat for arranging parties and who was bringing what for dinner. They were all very careful not to confuse the two after Ray sent a message about a hookup he'd had to the family chat. Ma had been on his case for weeks after that. Max had put his phone on silent when he'd come over, and he was regretting that now.

Tori, Theo, and Theo's wife, Maricella, marched up the stairs, all carrying big aluminum pans of food. Max ran a hand over his face and groaned at the absolutely gleeful look on Tori's face.

"You were our best hope for marrying up," Theo said, looking around. "Guess the Torres clan is destined to stay blue collar."

Maricella nudged Theo with her hip. "You said if I let you come, you'd behave."

"Let me come? Woman, you don't let me do anything. I'm the man of the house, dammit."

Maricella arched an eyebrow and Theo backed down. "Fine. You're the man of the house."

She laughed. "And don't forget it. Stop teasing your brother so he'll let us go meet his new boyfriend."

Max hoped Danny couldn't hear the conversation over Ray and Tori cackling.

"He's not my boyfriend," he whispered. "He's just a guy who needed help. Why are you even here?"

"Because Phil is on call and couldn't come, and Eileen has bookmobile duty today so she's working late," Tori said. "We're supposed to gather intel and report back."

Max hadn't been lying when he'd told Danny being an only child sounded great. God save him from his meddling siblings.

"Well, you're here, so you may as well come in and meet him," he said gruffly. "But he's not my boyfriend. And he's been through a lot today, so don't be assholes."

Tori grinned. "See, I told you he'd let us in if we brought food."

That *had* been the deciding factor. Danny needed some meat on his bones, and if you could count on Max's family for one thing, it was feeding you till it hurt.

"Don't overwhelm him, don't ask too many questions, don't be nosy," he said as he opened the door.

Sloane and Danny cut off midargument, both of their mouths dropping open as they took in the small mob at the door.

"You must be Danny," Tori said in what Max thought of as her teacher voice, the one she used when she was wrangling a classroom full of kindergarteners.

Danny seemed bewildered by the horde in his living room, so Max jumped in.

"This is Danny and his cousin, Sloane," Max said. He turned to Danny. "I'm so sorry, but when they heard what Ray and I were doing tonight, they decided to invite themselves over. This is my sister Tori, my brother Theo, and my sister-in-law, Maricella."

Sloane turned to Max. "Isn't this some sort of abuse of power? The last thing Danny needs right now is a parade in his living room."

Ray held a hand up. "Whoa. Max is just helping, and the rest of us showed up to help too. Back off."

Danny cringed. "Sloane—"

She whirled on him. "No. You let everyone walk all over you. Remember Christopher? Alex? Kade?"

Max had heard enough. "You should add yourself to that list, Sloane. Curious how you're so concerned about him, but I didn't pick up a trace of your scent or anyone else's in this apartment before now. Some family you are."

She staggered back like he'd landed an actual blow. "You don't know anything about my Pack. My Alpha would kick your ass for saying that."

Max straightened to his full height and crossed his arms. "I have nothing but respect for Alpha Connoll, and I know for a fact he'd kick *several* asses if he knew how scent-starved a member of his Pack was. How can he be comfortable in a den that carries no scent but his own? How—"

Danny held a hand up and stepped between them. "I chose to move out here. It's my fault. No one wants to make the trek. I'd see Sloane and my mother more often if I lived closer."

Max didn't comment on the lie in his voice. It was well-practiced, but the slight bump in his heartbeat was still there. Max wondered how many times he must have made that speech to be mostly convinced of it himself. He also didn't comment on the fact Danny hadn't included his father in that statement.

Sloane glared at Danny. "I'll see you tomorrow. Come meet me for lunch?"

He nodded, and she stormed out of the room. "And Danny? Expect a call from Aunt Veronica."

"Fuck. You told her?"

She leveled a glance around the room. "I had to. Come home to Manhattan. You know your mother worries about you, Danny."

Danny's jaw tightened, and Max was overwhelmed with the need to wrap him in his arms and soothe away the anger and hurt. But Danny wasn't his boyfriend. Hell, he only knew his last name because he'd had to take it for the burglary report. He didn't have a right to touch him at all, let along hug him.

"We both know she doesn't worry enough to actually help. Go home, Sloane. I know how much slumming it stresses you out," Danny said, his voice colder than Max would have thought possible for such a sweet, unassuming guy.

Hurt flashed in her eyes, but she left, slamming the new door behind her. Max and his siblings stayed quiet, watching Danny gather himself.

"I guess that confirms the door works," Ray muttered.

Theo laughed, and the rest of them joined in after Danny laughed too.

"Family infighting," Ray said with a grin. "Feels just like home."

Tori started uncovering trays and poking at the food. "Come eat, Danny. I brought some of our favorite comfort foods."

Max eyed Danny warily, expecting him to kick everyone out of his apartment. Instead, he broke into a wide, dimpled smile and joined her at the kitchen counter, listening attentively as she ran through what everything was.

"Is he really scent-starved?" Theo asked in a low voice.

Max nodded. Shifters and Weres were weaker when they were separated from their Packs. Going without scent marking for too long could cause loss of appetite, achy joints, headaches, insomnia, and a host of other symptoms.

Maricella slung an arm over Max's shoulder. "Ma's going to want to adopt him."

"She won't if no one tells her," he snapped.

Maricella laughed. "Oh, honey. I've always loved your optimism."

Chapter Three

DANNY'S legs twitched under the desk, itching to pace. He usually had his difficult discussions with his parents on the phone, where he was free to walk around the room to let off some steam. But his mother had ambushed him at the office this morning.

It had been a shock that she even knew where the foundation was. She and his father hadn't come to the grand opening a few years ago, even though they'd been in town. Stanley had come, though. The Cresswells' driver had been more of a father figure over the years than Danny's actual father. Stanley wouldn't have missed the opening for the world. He'd brought his wife with him, and they'd both gushed over how proud they were.

Pretty much the complete opposite of what was happening now.

"We've indulged you in this ridiculous experiment for too long," she said, looking around like she expected to find a crack spoon or a cockroach at any second.

The office was a little rough. But that was because he preferred to put as much money into resources for the kids as possible. He didn't have the funds to rent fancy office furniture. He hardly had the money for the rent at all.

He'd spent days scouring secondhand shops to furnish the three-room office that sat on top of the small community center the foundation ran. The biggest portion of his office-furnishing budget had gone to outfitting the community center with squishy couches, video-game consoles, and a giant television for the movie marathons he held on Saturday nights for the kids. It cost him an arm and a leg to feed the dozen or so kids who showed up for it, but it was worth it to see them excited over pizza and snack food. These kids struggled every day to get by, and the center provided an environment where they could let their guard down. His goal was to give them a place to be kids. It wasn't all running around at the full moon or doing other supernatural things—sometimes kids needed a safe space to sprout fangs when they were losing on Xbox or a group who wouldn't freak out if a movie made them laugh so hard their fingertips sparked.

"The foundation isn't an experiment, Mother," he said with more patience than he felt. He had a million calls to make today if he was to have any chance of raising money to replace the gifts. "I appreciate your concern, but things are fine here."

She leveled a glare at him. "Sloane told us your apartment was robbed. You could have been killed. Think of what that would do to your father. His only child killed in a slum."

Ah, so it wasn't the threat to his safety that was the cause for concern. That was so typical. She was here on an errand for his father.

"We both know you'd tell your friends I was killed in a boating accident on St. Croix or something," he muttered. He rolled his eyes when his mother bristled. "I don't care that I'm bad for your image, Mother. The foundation is doing important work. Necessary work. I'm not going to let kids suffer because you think anything below Fifth Avenue is a Third World country."

Her lips thinned, and for a moment real emotion showed through her mask.

"We care about your safety, Daniel." Her voice broke, and Danny was reminded that she was a messenger for his father. He'd never really talked to her about the foundation because his father forbade it. She was as much under his father's thumb as Danny had been. "Being isolated from your family—from the Pack—it isn't healthy."

It wasn't. But even when he'd lived at home, it wasn't as if he'd been immersed in Pack. The Cresswells were members of the Connoll Pack, but it was practically in name only. They'd only attended mandatory Pack functions when he'd lived at home, and he felt so different from the rest of the Pack that he'd continued that once he was on his own.

It was so bad that even spending the evening with *another* Pack had helped—this morning was the first time in months he'd woken up without aches and pains. Max and his family stayed for a few hours, eating and chatting. Even though the burglary had been a terrible blow, it had been the best day he could remember having in a long time.

Max was right when he'd said Danny was scent-starved. The way he'd reacted to all Max's little touches had been proof enough of that. But Max had been a gentleman and hadn't taken advantage even when Danny pushed into his space. He kind of wished Max *had* responded, though that could be the loneliness talking. He didn't want a pity hookup, especially since he really liked Max and his family. He hoped he'd have the chance to see them again.

"I'll go to more Pack events, okay? I'll start taking better care of myself. But this isn't about me moving away from the Upper East Side. You and Father have made it perfectly clear that you don't support my career. I appreciate you coming all the way out here, Mother, but I'm not moving back to Manhattan, and I'm certainly not closing down the foundation."

"You don't have to live with us. We've been thinking of buying an apartment for Sloane to use while she's in school. You could stay there. It's close to the agency—"

And there it was. The ever-present guilt trip over not going into real estate with his father.

"I don't want to work for Father."

She made an exasperated noise. "You wouldn't be working for him. You'd be working *with* him. He wants to retire soon, Daniel. You need to be there to take the agency over. You've wasted enough time, don't you think? You had your fun, and now it's time to grow up."

They both looked up when someone cleared their throat in the doorway. Danny stood up when he saw it who it was.

"Max! Did you need something? Was there a problem with the police report?"

Max ducked his head a bit. "Didn't mean to interrupt. I wanted to drop by and give you a copy of the report in case you needed it for insurance. It has the numbers for the officers who are taking over the case."

He held a sheaf of papers out, and Danny took them and dropped them in the inbox on his desk.

"I don't have renters' insurance, and it wouldn't be covered by the foundation's policy. It's just a liability rider in case anything happens to the kids while they're here."

"That's a shame," Max said. He reached into his pocket and pulled out his wallet. He held the bills out to Danny.

"Ray and Theo wanted you to have this. I'm sure my Pack will kick in more. Yours probably would too."

Danny's mother sniffed and frowned. "Daniel has better manners than to solicit the Pack for money."

Max ignored her. "My sisters said they'd be willing to help with a fundraiser or something. Maybe a BBQ or a bake sale."

"You will *not* be having a bake sale like some preadolescent girl, Daniel," his mother said, her cheeks coloring.

Danny closed his eyes and sighed. "Mother, you owe Detective Torres an apology for that."

Her eyes flashed amber. "I certainly do not. I don't know why you have a stranger meddling in family business—"

"Oh, I hadn't realized the foundation was a family business," Max said, eyes crinkling as he smiled. "That's so wonderful. I was just telling Danny yesterday that it has such admirable goals."

"It is *not* a family business," Danny said quickly, cutting off whatever retort his mother was about to fling at Max. "And my mother was just leaving."

"I most certainly was not. I'm not leaving until you come to your senses and agree to move back to Manhattan. That slum you live in isn't safe."

"Max lives in the building across the street. It isn't a slum, Mother."

Max squinted at him. "Your apartment building is pretty run down. It's a safe enough area, but I can't say I like the lack of a security door downstairs."

"You're not helping," Danny mouthed at him.

Max shrugged. "I'm not saying you need to move out of the borough. I'm just saying you could do better apartment-wise."

"See? Even this policeman thinks you shouldn't live there. It's not becoming for someone of your station to live like that. It puts a lot of pressure on your father."

Max quirked an eyebrow at Danny, and Danny gave up on propriety and started pacing the small room. "That's not what he said, Mother."

"I'll have Stanley come by your apartment this evening. That gives you the afternoon to pack up what you want to bring with you. You won't need any of the furniture, just your clothes and personal belongings."

He'd had enough.

"I'm not moving back to Manhattan, Mother! You and Father made it perfectly clear I wasn't welcome as long as I was committed to social work, and I have no intention of closing the foundation down. Nothing has changed. I was stupid, and I left things I shouldn't have at my apartment instead of getting a safety deposit box or something. Because of that bad decision, I've got a lot of work ahead of me and not a lot of time, so I'd appreciate it if you left."

His mother held a hand up to her heart. "And what happens if you get robbed again?"

"Actually, he wasn't robbed. His apartment was burglarized. Robbery means thieves entering while someone is home," Max said with a shit-eating grin.

"You stay out of this. It doesn't have anything to do with you." Her nostrils flared, and she turned to Danny, eyes wide. "Daniel! Are you and this police officer in a relationship? You two reek of each other."

"I—"

Max stepped forward and wrapped an arm around Danny's shoulders before he could say anything else. Danny leaned into it, his nose bumping against the column of warm skin above Max's collar. He smelled good, like sun-warmed grass with a hint of woodsmoke. He also smelled angry, which was puzzling. Why would he be angry that Danny's mom thought they were dating? Especially if his response to it was to basically give Danny a hug?

"It's pretty new," Max said, and Danny's heart skipped. "But I'm just across the street from him. I won't let anything happen to him, Mrs. Cresswell."

Was Max pretending they were dating to get Danny's mother off his back? Max must have some sort of white-knight complex. First he fixed Danny's door and brought his family over to feed him, and now he's standing up to Danny's mom?

His mother sat back in her chair. "Well."

Danny had never seen his mother speechless before. It made him a bit giddy. "If you don't need anything else, Mother, I'm afraid I have things to do."

"Where have your manners gone, Daniel? I swear, it's like you went savage when you moved out. Introduce me to your boyfriend. I want to get to know him."

Shit, he had to nip this in the bud before it got out of control. "This is Detective Max Torres, Mother. Max, this is my mother, Veronica Cresswell."

"Torres," she said, wrinkling her brow. "Are you related to Mayor Torres, Max?"

Fuck. Danny hated when his parents did this. They had to establish social dominance over everyone they met.

"Mother—"

"Yes, actually," Max said, flashing a million-watt smile at her. "He's my uncle."

What? Danny whipped a look over at Max, who seemed unruffled.

"How wonderful," his mother said. Danny didn't care for the calculating look on her face one bit. "He's certainly a credit to your Pack."

"We're pretty fond of him," Max said, his cheeks dimpling.

God, could this guy be any more perfect?

Danny nestled closer, and Max adjusted his grip, pulling Danny in tighter.

She gave them both a calculating look.

"You know, Daniel, perhaps I could talk to your father and arrange to replace the stolen items. Detective Torres is right. Your Pack should support the foundation. We could have a gala fundraiser. The mayor would come, don't you think, Max?"

Danny didn't know anything about Max aside from his name and that he was from a big family. And apparently his uncle was the mayor. His Pack must be powerful if his mother was acting like this. Why hadn't Max said something yesterday? Though Danny hadn't said anything about being one of *those* Cresswells either. So they were even. Kind of.

"Oh, I'm sure he would if I asked," Max said pleasantly. "The foundation does such great work. Uncle Albert is committed to making sure no child falls through the cracks, and Danny's foundation is the perfect example of putting the kinds of policies my uncle fights for into practice."

Danny barely held back his snort. His parents didn't give two shits about his foundation. They thought it was a waste of time and money. But apparently it was worth their while if it meant an in with the mayor.

His mother stood and smoothed her skirt, careful not to let her handbag touch the floor of his office.

"Wonderful, it's settled, then. Daniel, I'll expect you both for dinner at seven tomorrow so we can begin planning the gala. Your father will have a check cut for you for however much you need to replace what was stolen. Just email his secretary the amount. Max, it was lovely to meet you. Please give my regards to your uncle the next time you see him."

She blew air kisses to both of them and swept out of the room in a breeze of rosewater-scented air.

"What just happened?"

Danny rested his head on Max's shoulder. "You just got co-opted into the Cresswell family. I'm so sorry. I'll go tomorrow and let them know we're not actually dating. That will get you off the hook."

At least he hoped it would. A connection like Mayor Torres would be very good for his father's business, so he had a nagging suspicion that his mother wouldn't let something like the fact that they weren't actually dating get in the way of planning their wedding.

"No, it's okay." Max gave him a tight hug and released him. "If getting my uncle to come to a fundraiser means you can replace all those things for the kids, then we'll get my uncle to come to a fundraiser. He'd be happy to."

It wouldn't be a normal fundraiser. It would be a way for his parents to up their social influence and gain favor with investors in the city. Still, the foundation could use the money. Danny could suffer through this, but he wasn't going to drag Max down with him.

"I really appreciate that. But you don't know my parents. They'll squeeze you dry for every ounce of influence they can. You don't want to be involved in this."

Max narrowed his eyes. "So a Filipino cop from Brooklyn isn't good enough to mingle with your family?"

"What? No!" Danny pushed his hair back from his face in frustration. "Your family is awesome. They actually care about you, and they're interested in the things you do. My family is completely different. Dinner will be two hours of subtle digs at my career, my life, and the way I've 'frittered away' my inheritance. My father will harp on my decision to get a 'useless' degree, and my mother will bemoan the fact that I'll never meet a decent guy until I cut my hair/wear better clothes/ get a more prestigious job/move back to Manhattan or whatever else she can come up with. It will be torture. I don't want to subject you to that."

Max's face softened and he ran his fingers through Danny's hair, coaxing it to lie flat after Danny had spiked it up.

"Your hair is perfect. I like a little something to hold on to on a guy," Max said with a grin. "Your job is awesome, and you didn't pick the best building in Brooklyn to live in, but it'll do. Your fashion sense is crap, though, and I'm going to have to side with your mother on that one. But that's an easy fix."

Danny laughed and looked down at the foundation polo shirt he had grabbed off the top of the laundry pile and the ripped cargo shorts he was wearing. His socks didn't match, but his shoes did, so he was better off than he'd been three days ago when he'd worn two different sneakers.

"I dress up when I'm going out to see donors," he said with a shrug. "The kids don't care what I'm wearing."

Max shook his head. "It should be a crime to hide that ass under baggy shorts."

Danny's couldn't help but preen a little at the backhanded compliment. "You should see me in a tux."

"Sounds like I will, assuming this gala your parents are planning is a black tie affair. So, I'll pick you up tomorrow at what, six? How long does it take to drive to your parents' house?"

"You're really going to go through with that? Are we going to pretend to be dating?"

Max's eyes sparkled when he laughed. Danny's stomach swooped. He was going to have to be careful or he'd fall head over heels for this guy.

"What if it's not pretend?" Max asked, his expression turning serious.

"You actually want to date me?"

"Will dating me get your parents off your back for a bit?"

"About finding a partner, yes. Probably not about anything else. Though they might be on better behavior with you there."

They'd be focused on getting in on Mayor Torres's good side, and treating his nephew's boyfriend like shit would probably hurt their chances.

"Then it can be our first date."

Danny wrinkled his nose. "No way. First dates are supposed to be awkward because you're getting to know each other and you're afraid to order something messy to eat. I think people usually save abject parental humiliation until at least the third or fourth date."

Max winked. "Then how about you come to lunch with me? We can't count last night as our first date because I was on the job for part of it and my family crashed later. We can go get lunch and get the first date jitters out of the way. I'm not off till eight tonight, but if you don't mind a late dinner that can be date number two. I'll pick up takeout on the way back, and you can come over to my place. That way dinner tomorrow at your parents' is date three."

Was Max actually asking him out? Danny wasn't sure if he was teasing or being serious.

"I was supposed to have lunch with Sloane today," he said, his heart kicking up a notch when disappointment flitted across Max's face. "But her break isn't until two, so I can make it back before that."

"Are you sure? Because Sloane was pretty pissed off yesterday about me taking advantage—"

"You could take advantage of me any way you wanted," Danny blurted. "Shit. That sounded kinkier than I meant."

Danny grabbed his phone off the desk and shot off a text to Sloane letting her know he'd meet her at her favorite coffee shop on campus after class.

"How about we take things slow and see where they go?" Max said. "I'll be honest—you're not my usual type. But I haven't been able to stop thinking about you since you ran out into traffic yesterday trying to chase me down."

Danny flushed. "I thought you were the officer responding to my call."

Max grinned at him, and the happiness in his scent took Danny's breath away.

"I've never been chased before," Max teased. "I kinda liked it."

Danny decided to take that as an invitation to do a little more chasing. He leaned in for a kiss, moving slowly so Max plenty of time to pull away. Max's scent thickened and his heart rate sped up. He tilted his head, eyes fluttering shut as Danny closed the rest of the distance between them.

First kisses were usually awkward, and they didn't get much better after the newness wore off. Danny had never seen the appeal with previous partners. It was always just the prelude to something more fun. A step in the process he could take or leave.

But it was different with Max. He could feel the warmth of Max's lips even before they touched his, and the anticipation made his breath catch. The kiss was soft and tentative at first, but it didn't take long before Max took control. The press of his lips became more insistent, and Danny groaned and plastered himself to Max. Every point of contact between them made his skin buzz in the most delicious way. He'd never felt like this before, and it was intoxicating.

His head was spinning by the time Max leaned back to break the kiss. He had his hands on Danny's shoulders, and Danny's knees were weak enough he was afraid he might fall without the support. Max stared at him in shock, his eyes shining amber instead of his usual warm brown. He blinked and looked away, the glowing color gone by the time he turned back to Danny.

"Wow," Danny murmured, still trying to get his galloping heart under control.

Max reached up and traced the pads of his fingers over Danny's kiss-swollen lips.

"Wow," he agreed with a nod.

Danny let go of him and blew out a breath. "Okay. So that happened."

Max laughed and dropped his hands from Danny's shoulders. "We definitely have chemistry."

"If we had much *more* chemistry, it would be illegal in a public place," Danny muttered.

Max's smile deepened. "Let's go have lunch. I want to hear more about you."

This guy was unreal. Gorgeous, kind, funny, *and* he wanted to get to know Danny instead of rushing him off for a quickie? Hubba, hubba.

"You have to tell me more about your family," Danny said as he ushered Max into the hallway and locked the office behind them. They made their way toward the elevator. "Everyone I met last night was awesome."

Max lit up. "In that case, are you up for meeting some more of them?"

Max had gone toe-to-toe with Veronica Cresswell and lived to tell the tale, and then he'd kissed Danny until his brain melted. Danny was up for nearly anything he wanted to do.

"Sure. Will they be joining us for lunch?"

"No, they'll be *making* lunch. I'm taking you to Paulo's."

"What's Paulo's?"

"Homestyle Pinoy food. My Auntie Ginn owns it, and my cousins help her run it. You seemed to like dinner last night, so you should love it."

How big was Max's family? It seemed like every story introduced more family members. It fascinated Danny.

"Are they in your Pack too? Ray said last night your Pack was mostly family."

"A good number of them are. Shifters tend to form familial Packs. You're either born into them or you marry into them, with a few exceptions."

A niggle of disappointment bloomed in Danny's stomach. He'd really enjoyed hanging out with Max's siblings yesterday. It had been more intimate and *right* than being with his own huge Pack ever had. He'd never thought about leaving the Connoll Pack before, but if he did it would be for a Pack like Max's. Too bad he couldn't switch.

"You never told me what type of shifter you are."

Last night the question would have been unforgivably rude, but if they were going to make a go of this relationship thing, he needed to know, even if their dating was mostly for show. Once she found out Danny had gone out with Max today, Sloane would expect a full report, and his parents would want to know more about Max before dinner tomorrow too.

Max flashed his eyes at him in the empty elevator. "Binturong. It's a small bear. I have claws, fangs, and a pretty unsightly mullet when I do a half shift."

Shifters were different from werewolves because they weren't influenced by the moon. In terms of strength, speed, and other super senses, it depended on what type of animal form the shifter had.

"I'd like to see you with a mullet." The thought made him smile.

Max's lips twitched. "We'll see. That's fourth- or fifth-date status."

Chapter Four

"**I'VE** never seen you so nervous about a date."

Max tossed a balled-up T-shirt at his computer screen, and his sister shrieked.

"Are you going to help me pick out something to wear or not, Tori? I googled Danny's family, and they're megarich. Like vacation home on a private island rich. Get written up in the society pages rich. And Uncle Al laughed his head off when I told him I was working on a fundraiser with them."

"It's just dinner at their house, right? How fancy could it be? I mean, Danny is pretty chill. He didn't even have enough forks for all of us at dinner."

Max leaned over the computer and emailed her a link. "His parents are definitely *not* chill. That's their house. *Architectural Digest* did a piece on it two years ago."

He ignored Tori's squeals as he ducked back into his closet to find a button-down shirt that didn't have stains on it or missing buttons.

"Max, what were you thinking?" she shrieked.

"I didn't know!" he yelled back.

He should have listened when Danny tried to warn him. Max's family wasn't wealthy by any means, but they did okay. He'd been to tons of fundraisers and events when Uncle Al was running for mayor. He owned a three-piece suit and knew how to use a pair of cufflinks.

But Danny's family was an entirely other scale. What the hell was he supposed to wear?

"Would a suit be too much?"

"How should I know? Did you ask Uncle Al what you should wear? He'd know."

He poked his head back out of the closet. "He suggested my bulletproof vest."

Tori snickered. "Well, if they're all like that chick, you're in trouble."

"Sloane's okay, I think. Danny said she's usually really nice, but she was worried about me swooping in while he was vulnerable."

Over lunch Danny had told him Sloane was overprotective. Max thought it sounded more like Danny was bad at choosing boyfriends, but he wanted to withhold his judgment on that till he talked to Sloane more about it.

"Besides, his mom really dug in when she realized I was related to Uncle Al."

"Uncle Al has deep pockets," Tori said. "Why is it people with money always want more?"

"Danny said his father's in real estate. I bet it's more about permits and brown-nosing the mayor than money."

Uncle Al had retired from investment banking ten years ago and decided to take up politics as a hobby. His son Bert was the Pack Second, but everyone knew Bert was just biding his time before going into politics like his father.

"I've got to go. I told Ma I'd come by and help make dinner. She's got all the grandkids tonight."

His mother had the patience of a saint and definitely didn't need any help minding her grandkids, but she wasn't above laying on a guilt trip to make her children spend time with her.

Max blew his sister a kiss as she signed off, then dove back into his closet to make his final selection. He was due across the street to pick Danny up in ten minutes, so it was now or never.

Max brushed a spec of lint off his charcoal trousers and put them on. He'd had to get a few new suits after his promotion, but this was nicer than his work clothes. He slipped the vest from his fancy suit over a light blue button-down and examined his reflection.

Hell, he had no idea if this looked good or not. It was probably fine. July in the city was hot, so he rolled up his sleeves, taking time to do it the way he'd seen them do it on *Queer Eye*. No need for cufflinks if he was wearing it this way. He skipped the tie as well, because it seemed too formal.

He looked at himself again.

Maybe he'd bring the cufflinks with him, just in case. And a tie. And his suit coat.

Shit.

His phone buzzed underneath a pile of discarded shirts on the bed, and he fished it out. Danny's number flashed on the screen.

"I'm outside your building," Danny said when he picked up. "Buzz me up."

"I can be ready in—"

"Just buzz me up."

Max looked around his bedroom and swore under his breath, but he let Danny in. His living room was cluttered but not as badly as his bedroom, so he shut the bedroom door behind him and focused on making a quick sweep to grab coffee cups and stray socks.

He'd just swept all his unopened mail into a drawer when Danny knocked on the door.

Max opened it, his mouth falling open when it revealed Danny standing there in a pair of Dockers and a T-shirt.

"Yeah, that's what I was afraid of," Danny said, shaking his head. "You looked up my family, didn't you?"

Max flushed. "A little bit."

Danny laughed and stepped inside, moving past Max into the living room.

"My parents spend most summer weekends on their yacht in Montauk," Danny said. "I figured you'd be over here freaking out about what to wear. Not that you're wrong. My mother will absolutely judge the hell out of you. But at least you get to be comfortable."

They were going to *Montauk*?

"You could have given me a heads-up, you know," Max said, pulling off his vest and starting in on the buttons on his shirt. "I don't even know if I have anything to wear on a yacht. Jesus."

"Eh, as long as you avoid cut-off jeans and a holey T-shirt, you'll fit right in. There's no dress code at the marina."

Was that really a thing? Did some marinas have a dress code? What would that even *be*?

"I'd suggest khakis and a polo or something. It gets a little cool out on the water after the sun goes down."

"So we're actually going to be out on the boat?"

"Yes and no," Danny said. "We'll be docked. And never let my father hear you call his five-million-dollar yacht a boat."

Jesus. The thought of spending so much on a boat made his stomach hurt. He'd been saving toward a down payment on a house, and with Uncle Al's investment advice, he'd turned it into a pretty decent nest egg. But it was a drop in the bucket compared to that.

Danny nestled in close and kissed him, soft and sweet. Nothing like the frantic kiss in his office yesterday, or the fevered make-out session they'd shared last night after the movie. Max was off-kilter, the kiss making him feel like he was fourteen and hoping his siblings didn't barge into the family room to interrupt.

He followed Danny as Danny pulled away, chasing the intoxicating taste of him. Danny laughed and held a hand against Max's chest, keeping him from picking the kiss back up.

"We'll have to cancel on dinner if we don't stop," Danny said, eyes sparkling. "Do you need help picking something out to wear?"

Max waved him off and made sure the door was mostly closed so Danny couldn't see the mess in the bedroom while he changed. He also didn't want the temptation of Danny's bright eyes or flushed cheeks distracting him from the mission at hand. They were probably already going to be late.

Montauk was two hours in very favorable traffic, which a Friday night certainly wouldn't be. It would probably take them more like three.

"Sloane's on her way here, and we can all Uber over together," Danny called through the door. "Do you have any beer? Sloane likes to pregame family dinner nights. Not that we can actually get drunk, so it's more symbolic, I guess."

Max grabbed a polo shirt from his closet and stormed back into the living room. "Are you honestly telling a cop that you're planning to have open containers in a car? Really?"

Danny looked up from his perusal of Max's refrigerator. "I mean, we won't open them in the Uber," he said slowly, his expression puzzled. "It's perfectly fine to drink in the helicopter. And the pilot is a witch, so you don't have to worry about a human seeing us pound a six-pack."

Max slipped his shirt on. "We're taking a helicopter?"

"Well, yeah. If we were going down for the weekend, it would make sense to drive, but we're coming back tonight. I didn't want to tell you yesterday because I figured it would add to the freak-out. There didn't seem to be any harm in letting you think we were driving."

Of course Max had assumed they'd drive. In his world, if you didn't drive you'd have to take the train, and the train took even longer than the Southern State Parkway. Holy shit. Danny's family was rich enough that they could afford to fly to Montauk for an evening to have dinner.

"I was kidding about drinking in the helicopter. Sloane usually saves whatever she brings to slam right before we walk down to the boat. The pilot really is a witch, but it's a six seater, so we'll probably have company on the ride down. It's not a private charter."

"So this is normal for you?" Max asked, incredulous.

"Not anymore," Danny said, flashing him an embarrassed smile. "My father and I aren't really on talking terms, remember? But for Sloane, yeah. She doesn't like spending the weekend on the yacht because there isn't much to do up there, so when she goes for Friday night dinner, they charter her a helicopter. I haven't been summoned for a dinner in Montauk since I decided to go to grad school for social work."

Max was pretty sure he was going to hate Danny's father. And he was totally sure his own mother was going to smother Danny with food and attention when she met him. Maricella had been right. She'd probably want to adopt him.

Danny pulled his phone out of his pocket and looked at the screen. "Sloane's downstairs, and she's already got an Uber for us. Do you need anything else, or are you ready to go?"

Max couldn't remember the last time he'd felt so scattered. "I picked up some flowers for your mom. Should I be bringing something else? Wine?"

Danny smiled, his scent going sweet. "No. They've got a wine refrigerator in the galley that could put a kid through college. The flowers will be perfect."

The flowers were from a street vendor two blocks from the station. His mother would skin him alive if she found out he'd shown up for dinner at someone's house empty-handed, but he wondered if that was preferable to giving Danny's mom a wilted ten-dollar bouquet.

It was the thought that counted, right? He stuffed his wallet in his pocket and picked up the flowers. "Ready as I'll ever be."

"That's the right attitude," Danny said. "You'll never be ready for a Cresswell family dinner, so you may as well just jump in."

Max snorted and followed him downstairs. Sloane surprised him by greeting him with a hug. He gave her an extra squeeze when she thanked him for coming with them.

"Danny pretends he's above all this shit, but they really get to him," she whispered.

Danny scowled at her. "I'm more worried about Max. You know what they're like with fresh meat."

The back seat was a squeeze for the three of them, but Danny scooted closer to him, practically sitting in his lap. Max wrapped an arm around him, and Danny melted against him.

Max listened to Sloane and Danny banter back and forth with half an ear, the other half trained on Danny's heartbeat. It had been pounding when they'd gotten in the car, but by the time they made it to the heliport, he seemed relaxed. Max liked this side of Danny—pliant and splayed out along his side, a line of soft heat that smelled amazing and fit just right against him.

They'd had fun at lunch yesterday, and they'd ended up watching a movie over takeout at his apartment after his shift. He hadn't laughed that hard in a long time. Danny was the perfect mix of goofy and brilliant. He didn't take himself too seriously, and that was exactly what Max needed. There was so much pressure on him both at work and at home right now that having someone he could relax with was amazing.

He'd never been so comfortable with a werewolf before. Usually his guard was only down around Pack, but Max could have fallen asleep in the Uber if he'd closed his eyes.

There were two other people on the helicopter when they got there, not including the pilot. Max could smell the electricity on him, and he was relieved when the man wiggled his fingers at him, showing off the slim rubber gloves that witches often wore to prevent power surges. It wouldn't have been fun to have one short out all the electronics in the helicopter halfway there.

"We'll be in Montauk in about half an hour," the pilot said after he'd shut the doors and climbed into the cockpit. "If you have sensitive hearing, I have extra sets of noise-cancelling headphones you can borrow to make your flight more comfortable."

Danny reached forward and grabbed three pairs from the pilot. Max had tried noise-cancelling headphones once and hated them. They couldn't totally block out shifter hearing, and they made his ears feel funny, like they needed to be popped.

The headset Danny handed him smelled like ozone and herbs. Max sneezed, and the pilot looked back and grinned at him.

"They're spelled for Supe hearing," Danny whispered. "You won't be able to hear a thing." He popped his on and sat back in his seat.

So much for getting to know more about Danny's parents on the helicopter. Max put the headphones on and grimaced. Intentionally dulling his hearing was eerie. He was good at tuning things out, but this was different. The moment the noise-cancelling kicked in was almost a visceral thing, like diving into a deep lake.

It also sent all his other senses into overdrive. From the way Danny scooted closer and buried his nose against Max's collar briefly, he figured he wasn't alone. Max moved in his seat and reached out for Danny's hand, twining their fingers together. Danny's answering grin sent warmth pulsing through Max's chest.

The sense of comfort and need to be close sounded an awful lot like his parents' stories about their mate bond, and that scared him. Sure, Max wanted to settle down. But he'd figured that was years away. He didn't know what to think now. He'd told Danny they'd take things slow and see where they went, but his instincts were going crazy. He wanted to claim Danny and den with him. Hide him away from anyone who could hurt him and keep him for himself. He'd never felt anything like this, not even for guys he'd been in long-term relationships with. It was absolute insanity to be feeling that way about a guy he'd literally just met.

Max pushed those thoughts away and focused on enjoying the sights. He'd never been in a helicopter before, and even though it was dark, he didn't have a problem, thanks to his excellent night vision. It seemed like they'd just taken off when the helicopter descended.

"Are we calling an Uber to get to the marina?" he asked as they made their way through the small helipad terminal.

Danny shook his head. "My parents' driver will pick us up."

"Where does he stay when your parents are down here?"

"If they're not going to need him, he drives back to New York. Otherwise he stays on the yacht," Danny said.

The Cresswells did not seem like the type that would mingle with the help, so that surprised him. "Will he be at dinner?"

"God no," Sloane said. "He's a nice guy. I wouldn't wish that on him. The staff has a dining area." She dug through her purse and came up with two tiny bottles of vodka. She handed one to Danny. "Drink up. It'll make introductions go better."

Danny pushed the vodka back at her, and she offered it to Max, who shook his head. She shrugged and stowed it back in her bag. Their refusal didn't stop her from unscrewing the cap and chugging the other bottle. The fumes made Max's nose burn. He couldn't imagine actually drinking it.

"Stanley has been with our family since I was a kid. He and our housekeeper, Elva, spent more time with me than my parents ever did. Elva retired two years ago, but I still hear from her on my birthday."

"He came to Danny's graduation with me and Elva. Alpha Connoll came too." Sloane shot Danny a small smile. "That pretty much sums up our family situation, honestly."

She waved at a man standing in front of a town car holding up a sign that said Prodigal Son and Entourage, which told Max more about this guy than their descriptions. He liked him already.

Stanley hugged Danny so tight he actually lifted him into the air. "It's been a long time since I've made this drive with you," he said when he sat him back down. "Missed you, kid."

He smelled human, which was curious. Max caught Sloane's attention and pointed his fingers like claws, and she shook her head.

How was that even possible? Were the Cresswells so careful at home that even the people who lived and worked with them didn't know they were Supes? Poor Danny. No wonder he rebelled so hard against his family—there was literally no part of his life in which he didn't have to pretend to be someone else.

Stanley held a hand out, and Max took it. The guy had a firm grip. "Nice to meet you, Detective Torres. Sloane's told me a lot about you. I hope you'll enjoy dinner tonight and not let the Cresswells scare you off. It's been a long time since he brought someone home. You be good to him."

Max was glad Danny had someone in his life who would give the shovel talk.

"Call me Max, please, sir. It's nice to meet you."

Stanley slapped Max on the back. "Looks like you've finally found a good egg, Danny."

Danny grinned and looped an arm around Max's shoulders, tugging him toward the car. "Coaches his niece's soccer team on the weekends, volunteers at the food pantry, and he's nice to his mother. He's okay, I guess."

Max wanted to sink into the car's cushions and disappear. He couldn't believe Danny remembered all that. They'd talked a lot over lunch and dinner yesterday, but he hadn't meant to make himself sound like a saint.

"A regular Boy Scout," Stanley said with a chuckle as he pulled away from the curb. "I like him even more."

"He was one," Sloane chimed in. "Youngest Eagle Scout in the state."

What the fuck.

Sloane's smile was downright evil when he looked over.

"Danny has a huge heart and a Pollyanna complex. I, on the other hand, have a trust fund and access to a private detective."

Jesus. Make that two people looking out for Danny. Which was good, even if her methods were a little ruthless. Two was still way too few, and if Max had any say in it, he'd be increasing that number by at least one. Probably more, if his family was as taken with Danny as he was.

"Sloane," Stanley said, sounding every bit the stern father figure. "We've talked about boundaries."

"It's pretty standard fare for a cop," Max said, even though he didn't really care for having the tables turned on him. "We'll run people our partners are dating if they sound shady."

"He knows," Danny said. "His son is an officer in New Jersey. Stanley had him run one of Sloane's boyfriends, and he came up with an outstanding warrant."

Sloane buried her head in her hands. "He wasn't my boyfriend!"

"I picked you up at his apartment enough to make him something," Stanley muttered. He guided the vehicle into a parking lot, the wheels of the town car crunching over gravel. "You kids going back tonight?"

"Yeah, we want to limit Max's exposure to the crazy," Sloane said cheerfully.

"I'll be in the galley," he told them as they climbed out. "Just come get me when you're ready."

Max's anxiety returned full force as they walked down the dock. The boats were all sleek and gorgeous, a totally different class than the pontoon boat he used to like to drive at Uncle Al's house on Lake George.

He shivered when Danny grabbed his hand and pulled him in close. "It'll be fine."

"It will be a disaster," Sloane corrected. "But you'll live."

Chapter Five

DANNY had worried the helicopter and the yacht would be too much for Max, but he'd been a trouper. They'd been ushered up to have cocktails on the deck, and things were going well. He'd even fielded Danny's father's questions about his investment portfolio with grace.

But he'd looked absolutely panicked when they sat down to dinner. Danny wasn't sure what had freaked him out. Honestly, if he'd survived this long, there wasn't much more Danny's parents could throw at him.

He snuck a hand into his pocket and dialed Max. It was on silent, but if he squinted Danny could see it light up in Max's pocket.

"Oh, you're getting a call," Danny said. "He gets important calls from the station, so I'm going to show him out to the deck where he can take it, just in case."

Max shook his head. "No, it's fine, I don't want to interrupt—"

Danny's father waved away Max's concern. "I appreciate that, but please, do take the call."

"Uncle Daniel does it all the time," Sloane said in a sweet tone that earned her a sharp look from Danny's mother. "Business always comes first."

Danny nudged Max until he stood up and followed him out to the deck. Danny kept going, climbing up to the deck above and getting as much distance as he could between them and his family.

Pretend to answer your phone, he texted.

Max scowled at him but played along.

"Detective Torres here. What do you have for me?"

What freaked you out?

Max bit his lip and texted back.

I'm worried about embarrassing you.

"That's something worth running down," Max said. "Did the forensic report shed any light on that?"

Danny pressed a hand against his mouth to keep himself from laughing. Max was taking the cover story pretty seriously. It sounded 100 percent legit. If he listened hard enough, he could hear Sloane telling some gross story about her human anatomy class, covering for them.

You're doing great. Trust me, they like you. And they never like anyone.

Instead of calming Max down, Danny's text made him even more agitated. His heart was pounding, and Danny stepped forward and put a hand over Max's chest.

"I thought you wanted them to like you," he whispered.

Max grimaced and put a warm finger over Danny's mouth. Danny nipped at it, just because he could, and a thrill ran through him when Max's scent went thick with arousal.

"Did the techs make any headway on unlocking that iPhone from the scene so we could access the photos on it? Oh, excellent. How about the text messages? Anything interesting there? Can you read me the last dozen or so?"

Danny grinned and decided to be bold. He left his hand against Max's chest and leaned in for a kiss, which Max eagerly returned. He didn't let it get too heated, but it settled Max's scent and chased away the bitter tones of anxiety that had bothered Danny.

I just started thinking about what rich people eat, and I realized I didn't know what all the silverware on the table was for.

Ah. That made sense. Max had been fine until they'd taken their seats at the table. Danny was glad they were on the yacht and not at his parent's home in Manhattan. If Max thought this table setting was intimidating, he might actually faint at one of Veronica Cresswell's infamous six-course dinner parties.

Danny tried to picture the table, but he couldn't remember anything out of the ordinary.

Just follow me or Sloane.

That will be obvious and they'll know I don't know what to do!

The yacht crew included a cook, but it had been years since Danny had been up here, so he had no idea who it was or what they might make. His mother always requested simpler fare while they were here, which was good. There shouldn't be more than a few courses, and nothing that would be difficult to eat.

Just ask a question when the food comes out. Then you look like you're being polite, listening to the answer. Sloane or I will start eating if it's anything weird, and you'll be fine.

He'd never brought anyone home who hadn't been raised in this world. Sure, he'd dated guys who hadn't grown up wealthy, but he wasn't going to put them through the wringer with his parents. There were plenty of guys from the country club who would be happy to be his plus one at events back when he was still on the socialite circuit, so he'd never really put too much thought into how nerve-racking it would be to be thrust into it like this.

"I think your theory is a good one, Evans," Max said as he looked at Danny. "We'll go ahead with that and see where it takes us. Thanks for calling with the update."

Max took Danny's hand off his chest and squeezed it.

"Thanks for coming up here with me so I could take that call. We'd better get back. Your parents probably think I have no manners, keeping you away from the table this long."

Danny snickered and pulled Max along behind him as he weaved through the tight walkways on the way back to the dining area. Max wasn't wrong—it would have been rude to start without him, so his parents were probably sitting there eavesdropping, assuming they could concentrate over Sloane's endless story about a gory dissection.

Everyone perked up when they entered the room, and Sloane let her story wind to an end. The staff had probably been instructed to wait until they returned before serving, because as soon as he and Max took their seats, the steward came out with a tray.

"Thank you for waiting," Max said, shooting them an apologetic smile that made Danny want to squeeze his dimples. "Unfortunately, in my line of work there really isn't an off-duty."

"I don't imagine so," Danny's father said. "Are you in homicide?"

"Grand-larceny squad, sir. If I do my job right and stop a theft ring before anyone escalates to murder, it gives homicide less to do."

Everyone laughed. The steward brought around what looked like a prawn with curry sauce arranged artfully on a ceramic spoon. Danny picked it up and slurped it down in one bite, even though he could feel his mother shooting a laser glare at him for tucking in first.

Sloane seemed to catch on, because she followed suit, eating the amuse-bouche in one delicate bite. He and Max were sitting close enough that Danny could feel how tense he was, and he used the excuse of dropping his napkin into his lap to reach over and give Max's thigh a reassuring squeeze.

"Good man," Danny's father said. "I'm sure your uncle is very proud of you."

Max ducked his head. "I hope so, sir."

"Are you working a case right now? How exciting. Was the phone call important?"

His mother's question seemed innocent enough, but Danny knew from experience that things were rarely as they seemed when his parents were involved. He hadn't thought this plan through. If Max wasn't careful with his answer, everyone at the table would be able to hear the lie.

"I'm not at liberty to share details of an open case," Max said. He looked at Danny and winked. "Of course, sometimes close friends and family members overhear things they probably shouldn't. That's just a hazard of working a case after hours. I can tell you I'm working the biggest case of my career right now, and if I manage to run down all the leads I've got, you'll probably be reading about it on the front page of the *Times*."

There hadn't been a single blip in his heart. Anyone listening for one would conclude he was telling the truth. Danny had been up there on the deck with him, and he knew for certain that there hadn't been a phone call, and even *he* couldn't hear the lie.

That was masterful.

Max picked up the ceramic spoon and ate the prawn in one bite, and Danny let out a breath. His mother relaxed a fraction as well, and Danny sent up a prayer of thanks that Max had passed the test.

Max dominated the conversation during the next two courses, telling anecdotes about cases he'd worked and answering an endless stream of questions from Danny's father both about his work and his family, most notably his uncle, the mayor.

"This is certainly more scintillating dinner conversation than we usually have," his mother said as the main course dishes were cleared.

"It's definitely a step up from med-student chatter," his father added.

Sloane's lips twitched. "Uncle Daniel, I thought you were invested in my success."

"I certainly am," he said, arching a brow at her. "But that doesn't mean I need to know how to dissect a liver."

Max laughed. "How far are you from your residency, Sloane?"

"I'll be starting in a few weeks."

"That's why we're setting her up with an apartment that's closer to the hospital. Daniel will be moving in too, of course," his father said.

Danny would *not* be moving in, dammit. This was why he kept distance between them—if he let them in on the slightest thing, his mother ran with it. If he didn't need their help for the foundation so desperately, he'd walk out right now.

"I won't be moving anywhere. I'm perfectly happy in my own apartment."

Heads whipped up around the table, including Sloane's. He never talked back to his father, but having Max's solid presence next to him made him brave. He was thirty-two years old, and he'd spent his entire life either avoiding issues entirely or capitulating on things in the name of keeping the peace.

He hated that being with his father made him feel two feet tall. It was so easy to fall back into the old habits of keeping his head down and his mouth shut.

"I believe you were instructed not to come to a family dinner until you had finished your flight of fancy with that foundation and come to your senses," his father thundered.

"If you have a problem with me being here, take it up with Mother. She's the one who summoned me."

"Daniel, watch your tone when you are speaking to your mother." His father's voice was sharp, edged with an Alpha command that must be obeyed. He had a spark, albeit a faint one. He'd never challenge Alpha Connoll for the Pack because he hated everything to do with it, content to use his spark to keep Danny, Sloane, and Danny's mother in line.

Unlike every other time his father issued an Alpha command, though, Danny had no compulsion to follow it. No sick sense of dread in his gut at being controlled. Commands usually fell over him like a sheet of ice-cold water, but he'd felt nothing at his father's words.

"I don't appreciate it when she appoints herself the arbiter of my life," Danny snapped back. "We talked about this, Mother. I won't be leaving my apartment. I appreciate your offer, but I'm perfectly fine on my own."

His father's eyes flashed, which startled a gasp out of Danny's mother. It was so out of character that Danny almost gasped himself. He'd never met anyone with the control his parents had. Their social circle was almost entirely human—they mingled with the Pack only when it was required. It took a lot of concentration and an ironclad will to be able to hide so completely among humans. Danny had never seen his father slip before.

Then again, he'd never continued to talk back after his father issued a command for him to stop either. Normally he stayed out of his father's presence so further commands couldn't be issued. It was a night of firsts.

"We've entertained this childish fantasy of yours for long enough," his father roared. "It's time for you to grow up, Daniel."

Max's hand clamped down on Danny's knee a second before Danny made the move to stand up. He took a breath and resettled himself in the chair. Max was right. Standing up would only escalate things.

"My work is not a childish fantasy," Danny said, fighting to keep his voice even. "There are children in the foster system who need help, and I'm working my ass off to give them every chance they can get to succeed. I'm not going to give that up to go be a drone in your real-estate empire."

"I never heard you complain about it when it was paying your way through school," his father sneered.

Danny fisted his hands under the table, and Max enveloped one with his own, grounding Danny and helping him fight the pull of his shift. His teeth ached against his gums, but he pushed the sensation back and regained his calm.

"And you didn't hear me complain when you refused to pay for my master's degree in social work either. I do appreciate the advantages you and Mother gave me growing up, but I'm not going to work for you just because your balance sheet says I owe you something for bringing me into the world."

His mother's mouth dropped open. "Daniel! What has gotten into you?"

Danny hadn't realized how much he'd still been under his father's thumb until now. Maybe it was hearing Max talk about his own family and how messy and fun being with them was. He could tell how much Max loved them from the way he told stories about them—even though he'd mostly kept Danny laughing with stories about how terrible it had been growing up with so many siblings and cousins, Max had a warmth in his voice when he talked about them that made something inside Danny ache.

He'd had every other privilege growing up, but he hadn't had that. At least, not from his parents. He couldn't imagine what his childhood would have been like without Stanley and Elva. He'd probably have grown up to be the same kind of ruthless jerk his father was.

"I apologize for disrupting the meal, but I won't apologize for telling you that I won't allow you to force me to move to an apartment I don't want to live in. Perhaps my tone was disrespectful, but so is unilaterally making decisions for your adult son."

Sloane's eyes were the size of dinner plates, but she wasn't chiming in. Not that Danny could blame her. His parents were the executors of her trust, and they would be until she was thirty-five. She needed them. Danny didn't. He'd cut those golden handcuffs more than a decade ago, and he had no regrets. He'd been lucky, since the money his grandmother had left him had been in a trust that matured when he hit twenty-one. His parents hadn't had any say over how he spent it, and he'd used it to finish college and start the foundation. Sloane didn't have that option. Her parents had died before she was the age of majority, and all her wealth was tied up in that trust. Danny's parents had been her guardians for fifteen years, and she couldn't walk away from them like he could. Not with her med-school bills.

"You're right, Daniel."

Danny couldn't believe what his mother had just said, but she looked him in the eye and kept talking.

"You are your own person. And while I can't say it doesn't hurt that you don't want to be part of what your father has built, that doesn't mean you're not family. I was beside myself when Sloane told me your apartment had been broken into. Both because I was worried about your safety and because I had to hear it from her instead of you." She took a steadying breath, and between one blink and the next had her ice-queen mask back in place. "That being said, you are behaving boorishly tonight, and it gives me grave concern about going through with our agreement. This kind of behavior simply won't be tolerated at the gala. Do I make myself clear?"

His father's jaw was set so hard Danny worried he might be cracking teeth, but he kept his mouth closed. Danny had never seen his mother take charge like this. He wondered if it was as freeing for her as it had for him.

"I understand."

Max cleared his throat. "I know this is a family matter, and it isn't really my place to interject anything, but I think your son is amazing. He's built his foundation from the ground up, and it's doing really important work. I'm sure Alpha Connoll is proud of him, and Danny's a real credit to your Pack. It takes a special kind of person to dedicate their life to helping others."

Silence settled over the table, and Danny unfurled his fist and twined his fingers through Max's. Sloane bit her lip and looked miserable, and if his father weren't a werewolf Danny would've been worried about a cardiac event, given how red his face was.

His mother was her usual collected self.

"Of course everyone is proud of what Daniel has accomplished," she said dismissively before calling for the last course to be brought out.

The rest of the meal passed in stony silence, which was an improvement over the arguing. Sloane surprised Danny by deciding to stay the weekend on the yacht.

"Someone's going to have to manage the meltdown Uncle Daniel is going to have, and God knows it won't be Aunt Veronica. I'm going to do some damage control and make sure he doesn't eviscerate the staff."

"That's uncharacteristically kind of you," he said, narrowing his eyes at her.

She crossed her arms and pouted at him. "I can be nice."

"You can," Danny agreed. "You just usually aren't."

"Maybe you're rubbing off on me, Danny Do-Gooder."

He wrinkled his nose at the old nickname. "Don't take any of his shit on my account," Danny said.

"I won't. Once he stops and thinks about how investing in your foundation will raise the social profile of his business he'll be falling all over himself to kiss your ass. He really wants in with Max's uncle, and you're his ticket to that. Once he calms down, he'll remember that."

Joy. Honestly he'd rather be yelled at. Danny hated watching his father cozy up to investors and politicians.

"Really, though, I can handle myself. You don't need to stay here if you don't want to."

Sloane chucked Danny under his chin, leaving him sputtering. "I got you, sweet cheeks. I didn't have any plans this weekend, so consider this my big contribution to your fundraising drive."

"Hey, I'm earning this money like a good ho. They're pimping me out to all the summer parties, and I have to go and smile and pretend like I wouldn't rather be home watching *Chopped*."

"On my Hulu account," she pointed out.

Sloane gave him a hug and after hesitating a second, reached over and pulled Max into a hug too. He loosened up after his initial surprise, which Danny was glad to see. He wanted the two of them to get along. Sloane was a bit hard around the edges, but she was family he could actually stand, so he'd forgive her biting sarcasm and general selfishness. Her heart was in the right place most of the time, and that's what mattered.

Max stayed quiet until Stanley dropped them off at the heliport. They'd missed the ten o'clock, but another helicopter was due in half an hour.

Danny bought them both watered-down coffees from the vending machine and settled in on a hard plastic chair by the window to wait.

Max stretched out in a chair next to him, his long legs out in front of him. His Adam's apple bobbed as he yawned.

"We're even now," Danny said after he'd taken a sip of coffee. "I've met your family, and you've lived through meeting mine."

Max's laugh was loud in the empty terminal. "Oh, honey. You have not met my family. You've met a couple of my siblings on their best behavior and my favorite auntie. Your parents don't worry me—they might freeze you out over a meal, but no one has ever had to regrow a limb they lost over taking the last chicken wing."

Could they actually regrow a limb? Danny had never really given it much thought. Their healing factor was accelerated, sure, but did that mean they could regrow things?

"Like, an entire limb or just a finger?"

"Eh, half a pinky. Ray should have known better than to get between Eileen and that chicken wing. She was eight months pregnant at the time."

Laughter burbled out of Danny even though he was trying his best to stay serious and not let Max wave away hours of bad behavior from his family. "She didn't."

"She did. And Ma yelled at *Ray*, not her. Like I said, she was gigantic. Eight months pregnant and cranky as hell. It's a miracle she didn't kill him."

"Well, even with the threat of bodily injury, your family sounds like a lot more fun than mine."

"Speaking of bodily injury, should I be worried? Your mother spent dessert staring at me like she was mentally fitting me for cement boots. I know I spoke out of turn there, but I couldn't listen to them cut you down like that."

Danny sighed. "It's worse. She was probably sizing you up for a tux."

"You did a good job standing up for yourself. Is it always like that?"

"Dinner with my parents?" He thought about lying, but he and Max were really getting along, and if they were going to have a chance at dating, or even being good friends, it was best if Danny was upfront in the beginning about the hot mess Max was signing up for.

"It's usually worse, actually. This was the first time I spoke up. Normally I just stay quiet."

A bitter edge entered Max's scent, but outwardly he didn't look angry. Danny was going to have to have

Max teach him how to do that. He wore all his emotions on his sleeve.

"I don't like the way they talk to you. I've been to parole hearings where the inmate was treated with more respect."

"That's how they've always been. In a way, them cutting me off was the best thing they could have done for me. Without holding money over my head, they don't have any real power over me. I'd have walked out early in the dinner if you hadn't been there. That's how the last ten years have gone. I see them at full-moon runs and other Pack events, and I go by at Christmas. But other than that, I limit my contact with them for my own well-being."

"Family's not supposed to tear you down like that."

There was a faint growl to Max's words, and it sounded sexy as hell. Under different circumstances, a voice like that could get Danny on his knees. His scent must have spiked, because Max's scowl turned into an incredulous look.

"Talking about how awful your parents are gets you hot?"

Danny grimaced. "Of course not. But you sticking up for me? Yeah, that does it for me. I never really saw the appeal of the cop fantasy before, but I could definitely fantasize about you."

Max swept a glance over Danny, his eyes bright, and a spear of pure want curled Danny's toes. The lounge was deserted, but Danny still darted a gaze around, worried that everything he wanted to do to Max was written on his face.

"Is this—I mean, do you mean that? Because I know I said we'd take things slow, but I don't have slow feelings about you."

The possessive tone in Max's velvety smooth voice made Danny shiver, gooseflesh covering his arms. He'd never been attracted to Alpha-male types before. He liked to be the one in control. But nothing about Max was threatening—completely the opposite, actually. He made Danny feel safe and comfortable.

"There's a definite appeal to moving faster," Danny said, his heart in his throat.

Max's eyes flashed, and Danny swore he could see his teeth shift. "I should tell you—"

"Ready, guys? I've got the helicopter fueled up and ready to take you back to the city."

Danny jumped. He hadn't registered Devon coming into the lounge. He'd been too wrapped up in Max. He was glad witches didn't have the same sense of smell werewolves and shifters had. There were more pheromones in here than at a high school dance.

Max took a breath and nodded. "Let's get back. I've got to work tomorrow."

Danny hadn't thought about that. He worked all hours himself, since foster emergencies didn't limit themselves to nine to five on weekdays, but it wasn't like he had to be at the office for that. He should have insisted they have dinner earlier.

"That case you were telling my parents about?" Danny asked as Max fell into step beside him on the tarmac.

"There's a big theft ring we're trying to bring down. We really do have phones and computers taken from a scene we busted yesterday. The techs haven't gotten them working yet. I've got to go in and do some paperwork and make some phone calls tomorrow morning."

No one else was flying this late, so Danny nestled up against Max when they'd taken their seats. They buckled in and put on the headphones, and Danny must have fallen asleep because the next thing he knew Max was unbuckling him and tugging him to his feet.

"C'mon. Ray is waiting for us."

Danny blinked blearily. "Why didn't you just call an Uber?"

"Because if I was in a stranger's car right now, I might lose my cool," Max said.

It was dark, but Danny's eyesight was excellent. The shadows from the terminal didn't hide the way Max's nose kept flaring as he scented the air or the hint of fang peeking out from his lips. His eyes weren't exactly glowing, but something wasn't right about them either. It might have been a trick of the light, but his pupils were limned with a golden-amber halo.

Danny knew better than to push a stressed-out shifter. He let Max guide him out to the curb with a hand on his back, like he was herding him. Ray was already there, idling in a pickup.

"Do you—"

Max opened the door and pushed Danny in without a word. That answered his question, at least. He'd been asking if Max wanted him in the middle or not.

Max climbed in and slammed the door. In the close quarters, he smelled like anxiety and lust. It was an odd combination.

"Care to tell me what's going on now?"

Ray cracked up at Danny's question, which made Max tenser.

"You fell asleep against me," Max muttered. "That combined with how dinner went kind of sent my senses haywire."

"Haywire," Ray echoed with another laugh. "You two are attracted to each other. You want to bone. And Max's instincts want to put a ring on it."

A ring on—

"What?" Danny yelped, peeling himself away from Max's side and sitting up straight on the bench seat. "You want to *what*?"

Max growled, and surprisingly, Ray cowered away from it, his laugh stopping abruptly. He didn't look over to meet his brother's eye, but he apologized.

"I don't want to *put a ring on it*," Max bit out. "I'm just having some trouble controlling myself. You trust me enough to bare your neck and relax. It means a lot to a shifter."

It meant a lot to a werewolf too. It usually took months of dating before Danny could fall asleep next to someone. Most of the guys he'd been with took that as a lack of commitment, and they hadn't been wrong. It just wasn't a lack of commitment from *him*. His wolf was picky about who it would take its guard down with, but that wasn't something he could explain to a human.

"I think we need to talk about this, but honestly, I'm wrung out from being with my parents tonight, and I'm exhausted, so it's going to have to wait until tomorrow."

"Hell yes, you have to talk. Has he told—"

Max growled again, and Ray fell silent.

"We do need to talk, and you're right, this isn't the time. I should be free for lunch tomorrow. How about I come by your place with sandwiches?"

Danny ran over his schedule and shook his head. "Can't. I'm supervising a visit between one of my kiddos and her biological parent. We're trying hard to get them reunited, and the court has ordered these sessions to see if it's possible to ease back into guardianship."

Neda was a dryad who'd gotten hooked on meth. Her daughter, Leto, was a ward of the state while Neda worked her way through rehab, but it was much more difficult for a dryad to get clean than a human. Naiads and dryads were very susceptible to addiction. A lot of the Supes who didn't have high metabolisms like werewolves and shifters got caught up in drugs. They helped dull their other super senses, but synthetic drugs wreaked havoc on a nymph's body. Danny had a shifter doctor who consulted for him and wrote up diagnoses that human foster families could understand. Officially, Leto had a severe gluten allergy and allergies to preservatives. Dryads couldn't tolerate unnatural additives in food, and when Danny had met Leto, she'd been stick thin and sickly. On her new "allergy friendly" diet, she was thriving. She'd be doing even better if Danny could get her back in Neda's custody.

Max closed his eyes and leaned his head against the window.

"He should come to dinner," Ray said. "Ma makes the best lumpia, and Auntie Ginn said she'd make crispy pata, which is out of this world. Tori's even making macaroni salad, and she almost never does that. You really need to come. She probably won't make it again for a year."

Danny wasn't going to invite himself over, so he deflected.

"I know what lumpia is because Max took me to your family's restaurant yesterday, but what's crispy pata? And why are you so excited about macaroni salad? Every deli in the city sells it."

Ray snorted. "Okay. First off, that is not macaroni salad. That is some sad white version of it. Real macaroni salad is nothing like that watery shit. It has pineapple and raisins and cheese and there's like, ham and chicken and stuff in it. Secondly, I'm so sorry you've never experienced the mouth orgasm that is crispy pata."

Max cleared his throat but didn't open his eyes. "Crispy pata is not a mouth orgasm. Jesus, Ray."

"It's lechon—you know, slow-cooked pig?—and then they fry it, still on the bone. It melts in your mouth. It's so good you'll cry."

Danny's stomach grumbled, reminding him that he'd barely eaten at dinner. He'd been too on edge, and now he was starving.

"See?" Ray said, reaching out to poke Danny in the belly. "You need to feed your boy, Max."

Max's hand shot out and grabbed Ray's wrist before he could make contact with Danny's stomach.

It was impressive, since his head was still against the window and his eyes were still closed.

"Keep your hands to yourself, Raymond."

"It sounds amazing," Danny said, even though he wasn't sure about pineapple and raisins in a macaroni salad. "I hope I'll get to taste it all sometime."

Max opened his eyes and let go of his brother's wrist. His pupils weren't ringed with amber anymore, and his fangs had fully receded. He didn't smell stressed now, just annoyed. It was an improvement.

"My meddling brother is trying to get you to come because we're having a big backyard cookout since my grandmother is coming home tomorrow. She's been in the Philippines visiting my uncles for months, though I'm sure she's already heard all about you because every single person in my family is a terrible gossip. It's part of what I need to talk to you about, and I'd have told you about the cookout myself if my brother hadn't taken it upon himself to be an utter asshole," Max said.

He held Danny's gaze, and a ripple of *something* winged down Danny's spine. He couldn't label it because he'd never experienced anything quite like it. It was almost like one of Alpha Connoll's direct orders, except pleasurable instead of uncomfortable.

"I'd like it if you came," Max continued. "But I need to talk to you first. Maybe I could pick you up, and we could go over together?"

"Of course. I'm excited to meet the rest of your family."

He bit his lip to keep himself from babbling any more. Danny had never been smooth, but he usually had more game than this. They'd just met two days ago, and now he was talking about how much he wanted to meet Max's family? At least they'd already had a talk about this being a real relationship and not something casual. The wolf would have been out of the bag after a stupid comment like that.

Max's face softened, and he beamed at Danny. Danny made a resolution on the spot to make Max look like that more often. He was an easygoing guy, but he looked serious even when he smiled. This was something different, though. It felt private and special.

"All right, love birds, this is your stop," Ray said. He pulled up in front of Danny's building, and Danny thanked him for the ride before Max grabbed his hand and pulled him out of the truck.

"I'll walk you up," Max said. He held his hand out for Danny's key, and Danny handed it to him, giddy and indignant all at once.

"Are you opening the door for me?" he babbled. "Did I turn into a Disney princess on the way home from dinner? Am I Jasmine? I totally think I'd be a Jasmine. She has that independent streak."

Max grunted and pushed open the door to the apartment building. "You need a better lock on this. Someone could shoulder it open with no problem."

"You'd have to take that up with the building super. I'm lucky it was locked at all. Usually it's propped open at all hours."

Max glared at the door like he could change the lock just by looking at it. "You really do live in a shit building. Your mom's not wrong about that."

"No elevator, no doorman, it's practically a shanty."

A reluctant grin curved Max's lips. "I'm just saying when your lease is up you should look for somewhere better. I've heard good things about the building across the street."

"First your brother says you should marry me, and now you're asking me to move in?"

Max looked alarmed, so Danny took pity on him. "I'm teasing. I did look at your building, but I couldn't afford it. I had to keep as much cash free as I could because I was looking for offices for the foundation, so I didn't have enough for first and last. The owner here let me move in with just the last month's rent as a deposit. Plus it's like two hundred a month cheaper."

He stepped through his apartment door when Max unlocked it, and Max followed him in, looking around like he was hunting down a threat.

"I've been using the dead bolt," Danny said defensively. "I haven't had any other problems."

Max rubbed the back of his neck. "Sorry. Instinct."

Danny didn't ask if it was cop instinct or if it had to do with the funky bond they seemed to be forming. He wasn't sure he wanted the answer.

He leaned in when Max gave him a soft, lingering kiss that wasn't nearly long enough.

"I've got to get home. I have some case files I need to go over before tomorrow morning. Thank you for letting me spend the evening with you and your family."

"Thank *you* for not running away screaming. I had a good time tonight. At least, the parts where I wasn't being humiliated by my parents."

Max kissed his forehead and put his keys in his hand. "None of that was your fault, and it wasn't you they were humiliating—it was themselves. Lock up after me. I'll come by and get you about six tomorrow. Wear something a little grungy. A couple of my cousins' kids are teething."

Danny wasn't sure if that was a joke or not. He knew a lot about the supernatural community, but he had a feeling being with Max's family was going to be a trial-by-fire primer on shifter Packs.

Chapter Six

"I CAN'T find anything that ties all this together." Max's partner, Oscar, threw the file folder he'd been browsing through onto the desk with a disgusted grunt. "Fuck. There has to be something we're missing."

There was a lot they were missing. But Max couldn't tell Oscar that—Oscar was human. Forensics had gotten into the phones found at the warehouse they'd raided a few nights ago, but they'd been fried. Not just wiped—*fried*. Usually the forensic techs could get at least something off a device, but these didn't have anything on them.

Max was pretty sure they were dealing with a witch. It was hard to cause that kind of damage without completely totaling the device. The techs thought the phones might have been damaged in an electrical surge, though they couldn't explain why that would have wiped all the data on the devices.

A mature witch could cause that kind of trouble. Max wasn't sure if the entire ring was supernatural, or if it was one rogue witch flying under the radar and pretending to be human.

Warehouses all over the city were getting hit. Last week an armored truck had been robbed. The only thing they all had in common was a lack of security footage. The criminals seemed to know exactly when to strike and how to avoid the cameras. Some of them shorted out moments before the robbery, and others were covered or painted over as soon as the burglary began.

Entire warehouses were being cleaned out in minutes. The first one hit had armed guards on-site. They walked intersecting eight-minute loops. The thieves were in and out in less than five and had taken an entire shipping container of electronics without tripping any of the alarms or getting caught on tape.

It had to be Supes.

"Why don't you take a break? Get away from it a bit and maybe something will pop for you."

Oscar shot him a look. "You just want me to walk down to the deli and get you lunch."

They'd been at it since eight in the morning. It was after one now, and he and Oscar had gone over the forensics reports and the crime scene photos multiple times. They weren't going to find a link because there wasn't a link to find. Some of them were crimes of opportunity—the armored truck had been three streets over because a sinkhole had opened up on its normal route—and some were meticulously planned heists that were executed in mere minutes.

"I wouldn't say no to lunch if you were passing by." Max dodged the wadded-up paper his partner threw at him. "How about *I* go pick up lunch? And you can go flirt with Mahoney or something."

Oscar sputtered. "I'm not flirting with Mahoney! All I said was she did a good job on the report."

"Oh, Mahoney," Max said, fluttering his eyelashes. "You turned this around so fast for us."

"Shut up. I was trying to be nice. It wouldn't hurt you to make friends in forensics, you know."

Max hadn't cultivated any relationships there yet, but he was working on it, and not by flirting badly like Oscar. He already had an in with a witch in the morgue, and he had contacts in other precincts thanks to Alpha Connoll. He'd only made detective this year, so it was a work in progress.

Max palmed his cell phone and left Oscar pouting in the conference room they'd taken over for the case. He waited until he was a few blocks away from the station before he ducked into an alley to call Alpha Connoll's Second.

He'd met Jackson Berrings a few times, most recently a month ago when he'd connected with Alpha Connoll on Pack business. He'd spent the last six months meeting with all of the covens and Packs in the city on behalf of his Pack, strengthening alliances and making new contacts. He still had a few to go, but this case had taken over all his spare time. Pack diplomacy had to take a back seat to his job right now.

He liked Jackson. The guy was straightforward and really knew his stuff. He'd been an Enforcer for the Werewolf Tribunal before he'd gotten married and taken the Second spot in the Connoll Pack. Jackson and his husband, Harris, had invited him over for dinner, and while he'd gone out of duty, he'd actually enjoyed himself. Harris was a psychologist, and the stories he'd told about working with teenage werewolves had been hysterical.

"This is Berrings," Jackson said when he picked up.

"Thanks for taking my call. It's Torres. I have some case files for you, if you wouldn't mind taking a look. I think we've got a supernatural theft ring in the city, and I could use your help. I don't know what kind of Supe we're talking about, though I suspect witches at the very least. I want to get this taken care of before the fae step in."

The fae were one of the only supernatural species that didn't intermix with humans. They lived in a parallel realm and only came over to mete out justice when they thought a breach in secrecy had occurred. The Fae Guard were ruthless, and if they caught wind of the crime ring, they might investigate on their own. Fae justice was usually bloody and unilateral. They'd kill humans alongside Supes if they thought it was necessary. Max didn't want them in his city, and he knew Alpha Connoll wouldn't either.

"Fucking fae," Jackson muttered. "Sure, I'll take a look. If we can find anything that supports your theory I'll see if I can get the Enforcers involved."

If the crime ring was supernatural, Max would need help taking it down. He couldn't lead a bust on a bunch of witches with humans in bulletproof vests. They'd be mowed down with a single thought from a witch.

"Appreciate it."

"No problem. Hey, you want to come over and watch the game tonight? My Cardinals are going to sweep the Mets this series. I can feel it."

"In your dreams. Wish I could, but I've got a Pack thing."

"They play again Sunday afternoon. I think Tate and Adrian are coming over for dinner. You should come, bring your brothers."

"You're seriously signing up to feed that many wolves and shifters?"

"Harris makes a killer chili, and I was going to throw some wings on the grill. Nothing fancy, but we're used to feeding a crowd. Offer's open if you want to come catch the game."

Jackson and Harris had an apartment in Alpha Connoll's compound. It was a seriously sweet setup. The Pack owned the entire building, and everyone who lived there was either Pack or a Supe of some sort. It was about as good as city living got for someone in a Pack.

Max's long-term goal was to buy a place outside the city. Have a little land for the Pack to run, a house big enough for Pack nights and cookouts. Fresh air, less noise. A place where he and his mate could raise a family. He'd have to hang up his detective badge for that, but it was a long way in the future.

"I'll keep that in mind. Thanks for the offer. I'll have a courier bring over the case files for you. Are you at your apartment?"

"Yeah, I'll be here all day. I'll give you a call if anything twigs."

Max hurried the rest of the way to the deli and picked up lunch. If he was lucky, he'd have time to get the files copied and sent over before Oscar came back from his flirt break.

His afternoon didn't get any better. Lunch had been eaten standing over his desk, followed by hours of hunting through case files and then a trip to the latest scene to see if anything had been missed.

"There are cameras on every exit and in all the hallways. How did they manage to take them all out at once? They're not connected. IT guy says they just installed them—each one has its own power source. Every single one died at 3:37 p.m."

Definitely witches. This was the biggest theft so far. The warehouse had gotten a shipment of flat-screen televisions mere hours before, and the thieves had completely cleaned them out. None of the outside cameras were working either, and all the traffic cameras in the area had been fried.

Forensics thought the thieves used an electromagnetic pulse, but that would have disabled vehicles and other electronics in the area. The only thing affected had been the warehouse's security system and all surveillance cameras in a quarter-mile radius. EMP couldn't do that, but a band of witches could.

He looked at his watch and cursed. He was supposed to pick up Danny in ten minutes, and he'd be stuck on the scene for at least half an hour. If he was lucky.

Danny hadn't been lying when he said he was excited to meet Max's family. He'd smelled happy, and Max didn't want to ruin that. Danny deserved nice things. Max wasn't sure he'd put his family in that category, but Danny certainly thought they were. Besides, Danny was important. It was way too fast, but it felt right.

Knock, knock, he texted Danny.

Danny's answer was immediate, and it made Max grin to think he'd dropped whatever he was doing to answer. *Who's there?*

Not me because I'm still at the station, he sent back. He added a few frowny emojis because his nieces Jessica and Victoria told him they helped lighten up texts. Reading texts from the two of them was like interpreting hieroglyphics.

But he wanted Danny to know that he was sorry he couldn't pick him up. So… frowny emojis.

I'm stuck here for another hour or so. Do you want me to come get you and we can go late?

He laughed at himself when he realized he was holding his breath watching the dots on his screen that meant Danny was typing.

Wouldn't that be out of your way? Why don't I just Uber?

Max started to respond, but more text popped up.

I mean, unless you don't want me there without you.

Which is cool. I'm some rando you just met. Why would you want me alone with your family?

Max couldn't keep up—Danny texted as fast as he talked. He growled in frustration and stepped into the hallway as he dialed Danny.

"Don't be silly, of course you aren't some random guy I just met," he barked as soon as Danny picked up. "I just thought you might not want to be there surrounded by people you don't know. I want them to meet you. Why wouldn't I?"

Danny's chuckle made Max pause his rant.

"Well hello to you too," Danny said. "I should probably have warned you that I stream of consciousness text."

"How do you even type that fast?"

Danny laughed out loud at Max's grumpy retort. "Practice. Lots and lots of practice."

"I'm sorry I'm standing you up. I wish I could say it won't happen again…."

"But it will," Danny finished for him. "Trust me, I get it. Your job is demanding, and your hours are crazy. I can relate."

Max blew out a relieved breath. Danny wasn't mad. "I really am sorry, though. I was looking forward to a little alone time with you before the horde descended."

"I'm sure your family is wonderful," Danny said. "I'm starving, though. If I'm going to wait for you, I'll have to eat before going over."

That would be a tragedy. Ray might be an asshole, but he'd been right about the mac salad and crispy pata being rare treats.

"No, if you don't mind being there without me, go on ahead. I'll text you the address. Ray can introduce you around."

Danny blew out a breath, the sound making Max grin. "Good, because I really wanted that pig."

"I'll be there as soon as I can, okay? I promise."

He wasn't entirely fine with sending Danny into the fray alone, but he wasn't going to fight with him about it. It wasn't Danny's fault that Max's instincts were going nuts at the thought of sending him into an unfamiliar den alone.

Oscar was smirking at him when Max slipped back into the office they were using as a headquarters at the scene. Max ignored him and took a seat, eyes glued to his phone as he texted his brother.

Danny's coming over alone. Stay with him, Max texted. *Don't let him get overwhelmed. It's going to be a full house tonight.*

All of his aunts and uncles would be coming to see his grandmother. There were easily two dozen kids among them. It would be an intimidating crowd for someone who was new to it.

On it, Ray texted back.

Max walked over to the tech who was taking photos of a scorch mark on the exterior door. The lock had been blasted off.

"I thought maybe blow torch, but the burn pattern isn't right for that," the tech said.

The witches were getting sloppier, and it worried Max. They'd covered their tracks better in the beginning, but now they were leaving things like this. Other scenes had evidence of brute force, which made him think there were additional Supes involved. This could get really messy.

Max went in search of the manager. He'd already talked to him, but he had a few more questions about the shipment and who knew it was coming. He'd need an inventory sheet, too, and a rundown of the building's security.

It was six thirty by the time he came back out, and he still had no idea how the thieves knew exactly where the shipment would be. It wasn't dumb luck. Every time, they made a beeline right to their target. But so far he couldn't find anything to connect them. They used different scheduling systems, different delivery companies, different security systems. How were the burglars targeting these places? Where were they getting information about the shipments?

"You gotta get going to your family thing?" Oscar asked when Max rejoined him. He had one of the security cameras in an evidence bag to take back for the lab. Max already knew what they'd find—the thing had been fried. He'd bet anything that the wires would be melted when they opened it up.

"Yeah, I'm going to jet. You got this?"

Oscar nodded. "We're finishing up anyway. I'll tell the techs to call you if they get anything, but I'm guessing they won't process this stuff until tomorrow morning at the earliest."

Oscar had driven them over, so Max had a uniform run him to the station closest to his parents' house. It was a three-minute jog from there, and he used the time to try to prepare himself for what he was about to walk into. Danny had been with his family for almost an hour, so God only knew what state Max would find him in.

Max let himself in the back gate, closing it behind him in case any of the kids tried to escape. His parents had a decent-sized yard, by Queens' standards at least. Pack lived on either side of them, and the houses here were only a single story, so the backyard was fairly private. They'd put up a tall wooden fence when he'd been a kid. He still remembered helping to dig the post holes. Tori had been a menace as a toddler, and she'd been most comfortable in her shifted form until she'd hit about six or seven. Hence the need for the privacy fence.

Kids tangled around his legs instantly, and he let them climb over him as he made his way around the side of the house. Danny was faring about the same, with two kids hanging off his back and a toddler in half-shifted form chewing on his shoelaces.

"Sorry I'm late," he said when he reached them. He moved a kid from one hip to the other so he could lean in and give Danny a kiss.

"Ray said you were at another robbery," Danny said. "Was it part of your big case?"

"Looks like it." He scented each of the kids who had swarmed him and then set them on the ground. The kids who'd been using Danny as a jungle gym followed suit. "Go get something to eat, cubs."

The herd of kids ran off toward the deck where his mom and aunties were standing around chatting. His sister made a beeline for them as soon as she saw him.

"Lola's flight got delayed so she just got here," Tori said. "She's inside freshening up. Ray had to go get her because Phil got called in to the hospital."

That explained why his youngest brother had been nowhere in sight when he'd gotten there. He'd have to have a talk with him. He'd asked him to stay with Danny—there were a dozen other people who could have gone to pick Lola up at the airport.

The back door opened, and Lola appeared. She looked like she'd aged ten years in the last six months. Max wondered if she was tired from the long flight or if this was a result of the ritual they'd had before she left. She hadn't said anything about it taking a toll on her, but then again, she wouldn't have.

Half of the crowd gathered around her, and the other half—the ones with young kids, mostly—started lining up to fill plates.

"Is your grandmother the Alpha?" Danny whispered. "The kids were talking about how they couldn't eat until the Alpha came."

"About that," he said, sending Tori a death glare when she snickered.

Lola made her way over to them with her entourage before he could explain. She took his face in her hands and kissed both his cheeks, then did the same to Danny.

"I've heard a lot about you, young man. You've caused quite the stir. And you," she said, wagging a finger in Max's face and clucking her tongue at him. "You're too important to call your Lola? I had to find out from your cousin?"

She took Danny's hands in hers and brought them to her mouth to kiss. "It is an honor to meet you, Alpha Mate. My blessings on your bond. May you be a force of peace and wisdom for the Alpha."

The backyard was silent, and all eyes were on Danny, who had gone bone white at Lola's words. Max nearly swallowed his tongue when Danny bowed over their clasped hands. "My thanks for your blessing. May my hands and heart be guided by the Pack."

Max let out a breath he hadn't realized he was holding when Danny completed the blessing with the proper response. Not all Packs used the formal blessings, but Lola had always been a traditionalist.

The Pack broke out in whoops of happiness and applause, and Lola kept her grip on Danny's hands and transferred them to Max.

"You've found a good egg, Maximo," she said. "Now take him into the house and talk to him, because his heart is about to beat out of his chest, so I'm assuming you either didn't tell him you were the Alpha or you didn't tell him he was your mate. Either way, it's best discussed outside the ears of the Pack."

She turned to Danny and pressed a hand to his cheek. "Torres men are stubborn and hard-headed, but you've got some grit yourself. You'll be a good match."

Danny was quiet as Max took him inside. He didn't say a word until Max closed the door of his old bedroom. Ma had left most of his posters on the walls even though they used the room as a guest room when the grandkids slept over.

"Are you fucking kidding me?" Danny whispered, his expression fierce. "You're the fucking Alpha and you didn't tell me?"

"The room is soundproof," Max said in an even voice. His instincts preened at the thought that Danny was protecting the Pack by keeping their fight private. He'd be a good mate. That didn't stop the very human panic the stony expression on Danny's face caused. "And I was going to tell you. I haven't had the chance yet."

The excuse sounded lame to Max's ears. He sighed. "I started to tell you when we were waiting to fly home from Montauk, but the pilot interrupted us. And then my brother was being an ass, and I couldn't do it with him there last night. I planned to talk to you when I picked you up today, but that didn't pan out. I'm sorry, okay? It was shitty of me not to tell you, and it was even shittier to have Lola put you on the spot like that. I swear I didn't know she was going to do that."

"Alpha Mate?" Danny took a deep breath. "I feel a connection to you, Max. I do. It's different than anything I've felt before. And I really like you. But *Alpha Mate*? That is some serious shit."

Max rubbed a hand over his face. "I'm sorry. It's— I'm new to this, okay? Lola picked me as her successor, and she handed down the Alpha spark less than a year ago. I've been adjusting, but it's a lot. I thought I had everything handled, but last night—"

Danny's eyes widened. "That's what you meant about losing control. And that's why Ray shut up when you told him to also. Did you Alpha him? Wait, when you were talking to me in the truck, did you try to Alpha *me*?"

"Of course not!"

"You did! Your voice did something. It gave me goose bumps. You tried to use your Alpha mojo on me." Danny backed away from him, furious. "This is why I don't date guys like you. You always want to be in charge, and you get so territorial." He barked out a harsh laugh and threw up his hands. "That was what that whole scene was about last night. You being possessive. Listen, Max, I like you. I do, even though you're not my usual type. But I spent the first twenty years of my life with a bossy, overbearing father who wouldn't let me make my own decisions. I'm not about to become some Alpha bitch who caters—"

"Hold on just a goddamn minute. I didn't use my Alpha voice on you last night. Even if I did, it wouldn't work.

You're not Pack yet, and even if you were, it wouldn't have any effect on you. The whole purpose of an Alpha Mate is to balance out the Alpha. The Alpha Pair rules the Pack together. An Alpha Mate is an Alpha's equal."

That took the wind out of Danny's sails. He sank down onto the bed and rested his head in his hands.

"You said yet."

"What?"

Danny looked up. "You said 'you're not Pack *yet*.'"

Max shut his eyes and prayed for patience. "It was just a slip of the tongue."

"It wasn't," Danny said quietly. "Do you *want* me to be your mate, Max?"

Max sat next to him, relieved when Danny let him hold his hand. "I don't know. I mean, do I want a mate? Of course. I want to settle down. I want to start a family. And I feel something… extra with you. But is it the start of an Alpha Mate bond? I don't know. I've never done this before."

"Can I even be your mate? I'm a Were, not a shifter."

"We're not as hung up on that as you wolves are. And my instincts wouldn't have started the bond if we weren't compatible." Max frowned. "Do you want to stay in your Pack? Would *you* not want to mate with a shifter?"

"I don't have any attachment to my Pack," Danny blurted. His scent went sour with embarrassment. "I mean, I've never really fit in. And a lot of that was my parents' fault. They hate being wolves. My father calls it the family curse. They want to be as human as possible. Hell, they kept me away from the Pack until I Turned. I didn't know we were werewolves until I was sixteen."

Max couldn't imagine that. A lot of the Weres he knew talked about their inner wolf, but for Max, that wasn't the case. He was a shifter. It was his entire identity. There was no separation of human and shifter instincts—they were one and the same.

"I'm sorry. Do *you* hate being a werewolf?"

"No, of course not. But I've always been an outsider in the Pack. Even now that I'm on my own, I'm separate from it. I go to full-moon runs, and I come when Alpha Connoll calls a Pack meeting, but I don't have any real ties to the Pack. None that would stop me from transferring to a different one."

To *Max's*. Heat swept through him so fast it took his breath away. Danny had called him possessive earlier, and he wasn't wrong. Max wanted Danny to be his. His Pack. His Alpha Mate. Fuck, this was insane. He'd just met this guy, and now he was popping fang over the thought of bonding with him forever? What the actual fuck was going on?

Max tried to calm his breathing. He looked away, sure his eyes had flared. He didn't want to chase Danny away with some stupid Alpha-male posturing, but he couldn't help himself. His fangs ached, like the mating bite equivalent to blue balls. He wanted it. He wanted it more than he'd wanted anything in his life, and that was terrifying.

They hadn't even known each other a *week*.

Max pushed his shift back and tried to clear his mind.

"Are you still willing to see how things go with us?" Max asked when he was sure he was in control. "Even knowing that, endgame, I'd want you in my Pack?"

Danny offered him a fragile smile. "Your Pack is great. It's their Alpha I'm not so sure about." He took the sting out of the tease by squeezing Max's hand. "I say we keep on the same course. Try. See where things go."

"And if things get serious?"

Danny gave him a flat look. "Things are already serious."

That was true, but he didn't want Danny to feel trapped. Nothing was set in stone until Danny took the mating bite. Max's stomach rolled at the thought of Danny rejecting the bond.

"You know what I mean," Max said, trying to keep the desperation out of his voice.

"And if things get serious I'll consider joining your Pack."

"As Alpha Mate?"

Danny hesitated, cycling through several expressions before he spoke. "If that's where things take us, yes."

Max wanted to shift and run and roar, but he settled for smiling and pulling himself to his feet.

"We'd better get back out there before all the food is gone."

"I wouldn't want to miss my mouth orgasm," Danny teased.

His smile made Max's heart soar. He'd fucked up by not being up front with Danny about his Alpha status, but at least he hadn't completely tanked things.

"Crispy pata is good, but trust me, orgasms are better. At least, the orgasms *I* give are better."

Arousal clouded the air, and Danny sighed. "I deserved that."

"You did. And for the record, whenever you're ready to try out those orgasms, I stand at your service."

Chapter Seven

DANNY was going to need a shower before the day was out. Each pawn shop he'd visited was dirtier than the last, and he still had five on his list. No one would admit to buying a couple dozen iPads and laptops recently, and none of the stores had them out on display either.

Where else would a sixteen-year-old take twenty thousand dollars' worth of electronics to unload them? He certainly wouldn't need them all for himself. Was he selling them to people on the street? Had someone pressured him to take them?

Joss was a good kid. He'd been Danny's first case, a scared preteen selkie who'd gotten himself kicked out of every foster home he'd been placed in. When Danny met him, he'd been living in a group home, stealing sea salt from upscale groceries and spending so much time in the shared showers that the caretakers started putting limits on his shower time.

Danny had gotten him a membership to a Y that had a saltwater pool. Joss had stopped skipping classes and started doing well in school. He even volunteered as a swim instructor now, and he mentored younger kids at the foundation's day center.

Joss had been the only person aside from foundation staff and Sloane who knew about the gifts. And even the staff hadn't known where he was keeping them. But Joss had helped him carry boxes a few weeks ago. He'd been in Danny's apartment and knew exactly where they'd been stored.

The day of the burglary, Danny had dismissed Joss's scent because he'd been there recently, but after thinking about it, he'd realized the scent had been fresh. Joss smelled like salt and sunshine. It always made Danny smile, but when he'd stood in his living room and realized the scent trail was too fresh to have been made weeks ago, it made him gag.

He didn't want to believe Joss would do that. Joss knew better than anyone how much those gifts would mean to the other kids. But he hadn't come by the day center since the burglary. Danny called the Y and found out he'd been ditching swim lessons too.

It was so unlike him. Danny was kicking himself for not paying more attention to Joss. He hadn't been himself lately, but Danny chalked that up to regular teenage angst. He hadn't checked up on him, and he should have. Now it was too late. Joss was back to skipping school, and his grades were tanking. Most kids his age were hitting the books and looking at colleges, and Joss was out there doing God only knew what.

Danny had to figure this out before Joss got himself arrested or kicked out of school. But to do that he had to *find* Joss, and he was coming up blank. He'd been missing from the group home for more than a week.

Joss was in trouble, and Danny didn't know how to help him. But he did know that the first step was tracking down the stolen electronics. They were his only tie to Joss, and he wasn't going to give up just because the pawn shops made him uncomfortable.

He stopped in front of one that had its metal grate pulled down behind the bars, shuttering the windows. The neon sign flashed open, though, and the door wasn't locked, so he steeled himself and entered.

The inside was thick with cigarette smoke and dark— way darker than he could have safely navigated without his super senses. He waved his hand in front of his face to try to keep himself from choking on the smoke.

"Go away, we're closed," a woman's voice rasped.

"Your sign says open," he said.

She stepped out from behind the counter with a shotgun in her hands.

"And I say we're closed."

Danny held his hands up. "Look, I don't want any trouble. I'm just looking for some iPads and laptops."

She nudged the gun at him, and he took a step backward.

"I got some advice for you, kid," she said. "If you want to keep breathing, stop asking questions. I heard about you, and trust me, you don't want involved in this."

"So you know who has them? I don't even care about the stolen stuff, I just need to find—"

She jabbed the gun forward, pushing the barrel hard against his chest. "I said stop asking questions. I don't want you to bring this down on me. Cops are already looking hard at all the dealers in the city because of those warehouse robberies. Now you're digging around. Nobody's buying electronics in bulk these days. So you're not going to find what you're looking for in a pawn shop. Now get out of here."

Danny backed out of the store and hit the sidewalk running. He didn't stop until he'd put at least a mile between him and the crazy lady with the gun.

He thought about calling Max but decided not to. Getting Max involved would put Joss at risk. Danny had to get to the bottom of this by himself so it didn't jeopardize Joss's future. Hands shaking, he pulled out his phone and dialed Sloane.

"Hey," he said when she answered. "You said you used a private investigator to research Max, right? Do you think he could find one of my kids for me?"

"*She* can find just about anyone. Who's missing? Can't the state file a missing persons report?"

"They have, but no one puts too much effort into looking for a runaway foster kid. It's Joss. He's sixteen, and his caseworker pretty much said good riddance when I talked to her. No one's out here looking for him but me."

Sloane hummed. "Okay, I've got her info. I'm texting it to you. She's not cheap, though. I have her on retainer, so tell her to work this on my account."

"I can't keep letting you bail me out, Sloane. I've got a little money put away in a CD. I can cash that out."

"She's three hundred an hour, and a missing persons case can take weeks. You've got that kind of money?"

Danny's throat went dry. He didn't. But he had to find Joss before someone else did.

"Fine. But I'll pay you back."

"Sure," Sloane said. "By the way, Althea set up appointments for you and your new beau to have your tuxes fitted."

Tuxes?

"For the clean water gala on Saturday night? As in, four days from now? Ringing a bell?"

Shit. He'd forgotten. The morning after he'd cashed his father's check and ordered the replacement gifts for the kids, his father's assistant, Althea, had sent over a list of events he and Max were expected to attend. This gala was the first of several over the next few weeks. Apparently it was fundraiser season.

"I was supposed to pass the message on to you, so this is me passing it on. You need to be there at four tomorrow afternoon."

There was no use fighting it. He'd already spent the money. It wasn't like he could back out now. "The usual place?"

"Yup. You might want to warn Max that Riccardo gets fresh when he's taking an inseam."

Riccardo was about 108 years old. It was less getting fresh and more that he had to lean in until his face was basically resting against your crotch so he could see his measuring tape.

"Fine, but Max has a busy schedule. He probably won't be able to make it to the fitting on such short notice."

"Oh, he already knows. He and Oscar have it on their schedule. They'll be there."

"Why would Max's partner need a tux?"

"Because he's my plus one," Sloane said.

Was every damn part of his life out of control? "When did you meet Oscar?"

"When I went by the precinct yesterday to give Max the shovel talk and tell him about the tux appointment," she said cheerfully.

"What? Sloane," he said, groaning. "You already did that, didn't you? On the way to Montauk?"

"I gave him a very abbreviated version then. But that was before Alpha Mate Gate."

"Alpha Mate Gate? You're ridiculous. Don't call it that."

"Fine. You're no fun. But it's an entirely different talk from the regular don't-hurt-him speech."

Knowing Sloane, there had probably been a PowerPoint and bar graphs. Max hadn't mentioned it when they'd met up for pizza last night, though he wouldn't have. Not with his white-knight complex.

"Is the shovel talk a real thing? Max has like a million family members. Do you think I'll get one from everyone, or will they team up like an intervention?"

Sloane giggled. "Dumbass, you're not going to get the shovel talk. If anything, *he's* going to get it from his Pack. You're the Alpha Mate."

Danny knew that was a revered position, but he wasn't actually the Alpha Mate yet. Still, he'd take the protection it gave him. Some of Max's siblings were scary.

"I'm going to call your private detective. Will I see you before Saturday?"

"Probably not."

That wasn't unusual, since Sloane had a full schedule of classes and Danny worked long hours at the foundation, but he couldn't ignore the niggle of worry that she'd been told to stay away from him. His father had used that as a punishment for Danny before, and he wasn't above using it now. And Sloane didn't have a newfound immunity to his Alpha voice to hide behind.

"How long?"

Sloane was quiet for a long moment, and then she sighed. "Public and Pack functions only until further notice."

"Fuck."

"But he didn't tell me I couldn't see your boy. That's why I went over yesterday."

"He's not my boy."

"Your *man*, then."

"Ugh."

Sloane laughed. "I'll see you Saturday. We can talk on the phone. FaceTime is a no-go because he said *see*, but he didn't say I couldn't talk to you."

"He probably forgot that people use the phone for things other than business deals."

"Probably. Hey, do you think you can teach me how to do that thing you did at dinner Friday? Shrugging off his command?"

Danny had no idea how he'd done it. He had a sneaking suspicion that it had to do with his fledgling bond with Max. Now that he knew Max was the Alpha, it made sense. He remained in the Connoll Pack, for now, so he'd bet Alpha Connoll could still do it, but his bond with Max would have been enough to snap his connection to his father.

He didn't like being under anyone's control, but if what Max said about an Alpha Mate not being susceptible to it, he could ensure he'd never be under anyone's command again if he accepted his place in Max's Pack. It was compelling. Not enough to jump in without thinking about all the other consequences, but it was a definite perk.

"I don't think so," he said after a beat. "I think it's an Alpha Mate thing."

"That kind of undermines your argument that you're not part of Alpha Mate Gate, you know."

"I'm hanging up now," he said before ending the call to the sound of her cackling.

Danny checked the time on his phone and cursed. He needed to be across town at a custody hearing in an hour, and he had to stop by the office to grab the khakis and blazer he kept there for court appearances.

He decided to splurge on an Uber to give himself enough time to inhale one of the protein bars the office manager kept stocked in his desk for days like this. He didn't have a huge staff, but everyone was carefully chosen for the special skills they could bring. Not everyone who worked at the foundation was a Supe, but they were all part of supernatural families and in the know about the community. That way the kids didn't have to hide anything about themselves at the day center. It was a place they could relax and be kids.

The offices closed at one on Mondays, so everything was dark when he let himself in. He'd already shucked off his sweaty polo shirt and tossed it on the chair in his office when he noticed a bag from the deli around the corner sitting in the middle of his desk.

He picked it up, grinning like a fool when he saw the note written on the side.

Came by to take you to lunch, but Evelyn said you were out. Figured you'd be too busy to eat before court this afternoon, so take this with you to eat on the way. Max.

Danny finished changing and grabbed the deli bag. He'd been thrown when he found out Max's Alpha status, but he had to admit Max's behavior hadn't changed since the revelation. Danny didn't date Alphas, and he certainly would never have said yes to starting something with Max if he'd known he was not just an

Alpha but *the* Alpha. But Max was nothing like any Alpha Danny had known.

Even Alpha Connoll, who Danny had nothing but respect for, rubbed him the wrong way. The Pack loved him, so Danny knew it was more his own prejudices than anything. But he didn't like the idea of an Alpha being able to exert control over people.

He'd watched Max during the cookout whenever he got a chance, and it was clear his family loved him. Max had spent a little time with everyone there, and while it would have looked random to the untrained eye, Danny had noticed that he'd meticulously worked his way through the crowd, spending more time with those who needed him more. He'd scent marked everyone and made sure everyone had gotten enough to eat. Danny overheard him settle four disputes and break up one serious argument, all without raising his voice or resorting to using his Alpha coercion.

Max was wonderful. But Danny had to be sure before he let things get more serious—he had to be absolutely positive that Max wasn't going to become an Alpha asshole if they were together.

Danny ran his fingers over the note on the bag as he headed out to court. Making sure he ate was an Alpha thing to do, but it was also sweet and thoughtful. He could get used to *that* kind of Alpha treatment.

DANNY'S Tuesday had gotten off to a rocky start when he'd woken up in a pool of his own sweat because the window air-conditioning unit in his bedroom was on the fritz again. He left a message for the super and stepped into the shower only to find the hot water was out too.

He'd had two social workers deny him consultation on kids he'd flagged as potential Supes this morning, and

Evelyn was out with the flu, so he couldn't find half the files he needed for his afternoon appointments.

It had been a shit day, and now he was going in for a tux fitting with the most touchy-feely tailor in Manhattan. At least he'd get to see Max. There had been another robbery last night, another armored car, and this time someone had been hurt. The driver was in a coma, and doctors were puzzled. Max had missed dinner last night because he'd been at the hospital, and he hadn't responded to any of Danny's whiny texts about his no-good, terrible Tuesday either.

He was surprised when he entered the shop ten minutes before their appointments and Max was already up on the dais with a tape measure buried in his crotch. Oscar was sitting in a chair looking over case files, his suit coat draped over the back of it and his tie undone.

"Riccardo got us in early," Max said, nodding toward the little old man who had his face practically pressed against Max's junk.

Danny had a burst of irrational jealousy. He caught himself before he growled, but Max must have picked up on a chemosignal because he snickered and sent Danny a heated look.

True, he wanted to take things slow, but there was slow and there was glacial. But this wasn't his average boyfriend, and taking their relationship further physically had actual ramifications. The bond would react, and who knew what effect it would have. Danny was afraid Max would lose himself to his instincts and give him the mating bite in the heat of the moment, and something like that couldn't be undone.

"We're due back at the precinct for some more interviews in half an hour," Max said, his tone apologetic.

So much for having some time together. Danny had been looking forward to seeing Max all day.

"Are you going home from here or heading back to the office?"

Danny shrugged. He'd planned to invite himself over to Max's for the air-conditioning and maybe order food. With their relationship moving at warp speed thanks to the bond, Danny figured it was time to give up on the idea of taking their physical relationship slow. Who were they kidding? The bond was half-formed. Neither of them was going to walk away from that.

"I'll probably go home."

There wasn't anything that needed his attention at the office, and the center closed at five on Tuesdays, so there was no point in heading there after this.

Riccardo hissed out a warning to Max through a mouthful of pins, and Max stopped, face guilty, as he held his phone.

"Is it okay if Theo comes by to look at your window unit? I'll come over after I wrap up at the precinct. Maybe we can all order in dinner?"

And just like that, Danny's funk from his no-good, terrible Tuesday dissipated. Warmth spread through him like a physical hug—Max was taking care of him like he was one of his Pack. Instead of feeling smothered, Danny liked it. He especially liked that Max was asking permission instead of steamrolling him like he had with the door repair.

"That would be awesome. I was wondering how I'd get any sleep tonight."

The super had called and told him the AC unit was his responsibility, even though it had been there when he moved in. The last tenant had left it, so it didn't technically come as part of the apartment. Danny didn't know the first thing about how to repair a window unit, nor did he have the spare cash to buy a new one.

"Is he bringing Maricella?"

Danny liked all of Max's relatives, but Maricella was his favorite. She didn't tease as much as Tori or Ray, and everyone listened to her. He hadn't met Phil yet, but he sounded like a cool guy. His wife and kids had been at the Pack cookout, and Danny had liked them a lot.

"You want him to bring Maricella, or you want him to bring Maricella's adobo?"

Danny cracked up. "You've gotten me hooked on that stuff. But I was hoping to see her, food or not. She had an idea for using hemp fabric to make clothes for some of my kids who are sensitive to synthetic fibers. We've been buying cotton for them, but even that causes rashes."

Maricella designed wedding dresses, but she'd offered to make a few outfits for his naiad and dryad kids to see if hemp might be better for their skin.

Max's scent went sharp for a moment before it leveled back out. He'd had a spike of some emotion, but Danny couldn't figure out what. It hadn't been arousal—Danny was well-acquainted with that smell. It had been something more like... jealousy?

Was Max jealous of his own Pack members because Danny wanted to spend time with them? He waited to see if Max would say anything, but he didn't. He was ignoring whatever possessive, bone-headed Alpha instinct had caused his brief unhappiness.

"I can see if Maricella is free," he said after Riccardo had finished with his inseam and moved on to his sleeves. "She isn't working the long hours she used to because the baby makes her tired. She may be home."

Shit. Guilt tugged at his belly. He hadn't thought about dragging her out after work.

"I can call her later if she's too tired. I don't want her to exhaust herself on this project—it's a good idea, but I can get a different seamstress to do it if it's—"

"She'd kill me if she knew I opened my mouth about her being tired," Max said. "I'm sure she wouldn't have offered to make the clothes if she didn't think she'd have the energy. She's told me more than once that pregnancy isn't a disability. She's a grown-up. She'll let you know if you're putting her out."

"What time do you think you'll be done? I can order food."

"I'll bring something when I come. I should be finished around seven. I'll text to see what you want," Max said. Riccardo helped down off the dais and eased the tuxedo coat off him. Even full of chalk and pins, it looked great.

Max shrugged his suit coat on, and Oscar stood up, ready to leave. Danny let Max give him a quick kiss on the way out. It was like something an old married couple would do, and the thought made him laugh. If they were going to act like old marrieds, maybe it was time to push the glacier ahead a few paces and graduate past the make-out sessions that were leaving him with blue balls like a teenager.

Chapter Eight

MAX growled and tossed his mangled bow tie on the desk. "This is hopeless."

Danny poked his head out of the bathroom where he'd been doing something to his hair that involved more products than Max had ever seen in one place.

"Let me," he said, coming to Max's rescue.

Danny's parents insisted on renting a room for them at the gala hotel for the night so they could get ready on-site. It had seemed silly, at least until he'd seen Danny and his arsenal of hair products.

Max had picked up their tuxedos this morning, and his ego chafed a bit that Danny's parents had already paid for them. So showing up and finding that the hotel "room" they'd booked—and prepaid—was an enormous suite had set his teeth on edge. Danny didn't seem bothered by it. He'd waltzed in like he'd stayed here a hundred times before and asked the bellhop to uncork the champagne chilling in the living room before he left.

It was easy to forget that Danny grew up in places like this. He was down to earth and easy to talk to, and if left to his own devices, he'd eat ramen every day and wear his clothes till they were riddled with holes.

It was hard to reconcile that Danny with the one who looked perfectly at home in a tuxedo sipping on three-hundred-dollar champagne.

Max couldn't give Danny this kind of life. The bond was pushing him to show Danny how well he could provide for him and protect him, but what Max could provide for him wouldn't hold a candle to the life he could have if he worked things out with his parents.

Danny stepped up behind him in the gilt-edged mirror. His fingers moved effortlessly through the steps of tying a perfect bow tie. Max had spent an hour watching tutorials on YouTube this morning, and he hadn't been able to come close.

"There," Danny said, straightening it with a grin. "Perfect."

Riccardo had outdone himself with Danny's tuxedo. It was tailored to emphasize his broad shoulders and tapered waist. Danny had legs for days and the most perfect ass Max had ever seen.

As good as he looked in the tuxedo, Max couldn't wait to see him out of it. The universe had been a giant cockblock all week. Theo and Maricella stayed till after midnight Tuesday, and Max left when they did. Between Max's brutal schedule as he worked his case and Danny's evening hours at the center, they hadn't had another night together until now.

Max wished they had time to take the edge off before the gala, because the way Danny looked and smelled was torture. He wanted to peel that tuxedo off him and spend hours messing up his perfect hair, putting the hotel room to good use.

"We'd better get down there," Danny said. "Dinner will start in about half an hour, and Father will want to parade us around during happy hour first."

He hadn't thought about navigating the bar. Shit. What was an appropriately waspy drink order? Max preferred IPAs and usually drank whatever was on sale when he went to the store. At dinner with Danny's parents, there'd been a bottle of wine already opened, and he hadn't had to choose anything. He had no idea what to order here that wouldn't draw attention or embarrass Danny's family.

They took the elevator down to the ballroom, and Max tried to come up with a strategy for blending in. He couldn't always rely on following Danny's lead like he had at dinner. Max needed a primer in rubbing elbows with the rich and entitled.

"What does your father drink?"

Danny had been scanning the crowd, but he turned back to Max made a face. "Unless it's wine with dinner, he drinks scotch neat, generally. Why?"

"I figured I should buy him a drink."

Danny gave him a sideways glance. "You're being weird."

"The man laid down ten grand for a table! I should buy him a drink at least."

Danny rolled his eyes. "It's a limited bar. They're serving some weird coconut-water cocktail a local celebrity bartender made up for the event and a few types of beer and wine. You can buy him an overpriced drink if you want, but he's probably already nursing one of the house cocktails to show he's a good sport, even though he'd never drink it. They'll bring wine around once we're seated, and he won't actually drink until then."

Max would take a raucous Torres family meal over this any day. But he was here to support Danny, and that meant being on his best behavior and not adding to Danny's stress by freaking out.

He held out an arm and grinned when Danny took it. He liked having Danny close where he could make sure nothing happened to him.

"Would *you* like a drink before dinner?"

Sloane teetered over to them before Danny could answer. She towered above Oscar in heels that had to be four or five inches tall, putting her a few inches over him. They didn't look particularly comfortable or easy to walk in, given her mincing steps and the way Oscar was following along behind her, ready to catch her if she fell.

"Max! It's so good to see you," she bubbled as she leaned in to kiss his cheek. Her coconut-water cocktail slopped onto the floor, and she swiped at it with her foot, knocking herself off balance and falling against Max's chest like she was tipsy.

"You're cutting it close," she murmured when he wrapped his arms around her to right her. "Uncle Daniel is on the warpath because the mayor was supposed to be here to hand out an award and he's not here yet."

"He's not coming for dinner. He'll be here in time to give it to them and say a few words, but he thinks this is a sham of an award, and he didn't want to be in all the publicity photos."

Uncle Al was presenting some award to a company that had reduced its carbon footprint by more than half in the last year, but Uncle Al said it was still one of the city's top polluters.

He'd promised Max that he'd stay for a bit afterward so Max could introduce him to Danny's parents. It had been one of the conditions of their donation, and Max wanted to get it over with sooner rather than later.

"Well, the Clean Water Initiative board won't be happy to hear that," she said.

"Your uncle's a member, I take it?"

She grinned at him and stepped back out of his embrace. "President, of course."

Oscar was grinning ear to ear when she sidled up next to him. He slipped an arm around her waist but let her guide them through the crowd. Max had never seen his partner so smitten.

Danny flagged down a waiter to clean up Sloane's drink, and he took Max's hand and tugged him toward the dining room.

"What was that about?" Danny asked as they joined the line for the bar.

"Your father is upset that Uncle Al isn't here yet. She was warning me."

He'd definitely judged Sloane wrong when they first met. He'd dismissed her as rude, privileged, and vapid, but privileged was the only one that stuck. And he couldn't very well hold that against her while he was dating Danny, someone so clueless that he honestly didn't see anything strange about taking a helicopter to Montauk for dinner.

"He won't make a scene here," Danny said with an apologetic shrug. "Even if his reputation wasn't on the line, Alpha Connoll is here, and he behaves pretty well around him."

Fire shivered down Max's spine, pooling in his stomach. It was almost the same sensation as his skin rippling when he changed, but the pain was absent. This wasn't bones and sinew reknitting themselves into something new—it was more like his instincts rebelling against Danny reminding him that he belonged to a different Alpha. Fledgling bond or not, Max didn't have any claim over him, and it was making his instincts go nuts.

He'd known the Alpha was here. Even if Danny hadn't told him, he'd have known the moment he walked into the room and been enveloped by the raw animal energy of another powerful Alpha. Sometimes he'd even get a zing off an Alpha who didn't hold the Pack power. Shaking Mr. Cresswell's hand made his fingers tingle. Doing the same with Alpha Connoll would actually hurt.

Danny ran a hand up his arm, his eyes locked on Max's face. "Are you okay? Is it a problem that he's here?"

It shouldn't be. Alpha Connoll wasn't a threat to his mating with Danny. The man was happily mated himself and had no interest in Danny, but knowing that Alpha Connoll could put Danny on his knees if he wanted to made Max want to roar out a challenge for him right there.

Danny leaned in and buried his face against Max's neck. The contact soothed some of the fire in Max's belly, and he brought a hand up automatically to rest against Danny's back, encouraging him to stay where he was. Danny chuckled and pressed a light kiss to Max's neck.

"Is this because of some Alpha asshole shit?"

His frankness startled a laugh out of Max. It was indeed because of some Alpha asshole shit. He loved the way Danny could cut to the heart of things and defuse his anxiety in seconds.

He pulled away and met Danny's questioning gaze. "I'm not asking you to do it now because I know we're nowhere near there yet. But if things between us work out, would you be comfortable leaving your Pack to join mine?"

He'd expected Danny to shy away from the question or even physically back away from him, since he'd made it clear he didn't like Alpha types and hated the idea of being under anyone's control. Max was aware he sounded like a possessive boyfriend right now, but he couldn't help it.

Danny didn't move except to tighten his grip on Max's forearm. "Honestly? I'd join your Pack tomorrow if the only way in wasn't marriage. I love being with your family, Max. They're great. Did you know your Auntie Ruth is making me a sweater? For the winter. She said I was too skinny and pulled a skein of yarn out of her bag and started knitting one right away. For me, someone she'd just met. She was so sweet and kind, making sure I got enough to eat and introducing me around when Ray and Tori were busy. I can't even explain what it feels like to be with your Pack, Max. I've never felt so accepted in my life."

Max was staggered by the sincerity in Danny's tone. He'd only known this man a few weeks, but Danny had wormed his way into every part of Max's life. His partner liked him. His family loved him. His Pack was offering to clothe him for the winter. He was perfect.

Max pulled Danny out of line and found them a secluded spot where they wouldn't be overheard.

"You know she's not really my aunt, right?"

"She didn't smell the same way you do, so I figured. A different type of shifter?"

"Ruth's shifted form is a lynx," Max said. "She's been part of the Pack longer than I've been alive. She's also never been married."

Danny's eyes narrowed in confusion. "But you said the only way in was to be born into it or marry into it."

"I haven't taken in any new members since I took over the Alpha mantle," Max explained. "There are probably close to a hundred and fifty members. My grandmother did this full time, but I want a career. I want an identity outside of being the Alpha. So I decided when I took over that we wouldn't be taking new members unless they married in. But I was wrong. We've always been a safe haven for any shifter who needed a Pack home, and now I understand why. If you want to join, Danny, you can. You don't have to be my Alpha Mate, and you certainly don't have to marry me just so you can have a Pack that accepts you. We can have the ceremony at the next moon if you want."

Danny's scent went citrusy with surprise. "Max, you barely know me—"

"I know you well enough to be positive you'd be an asset to any Pack. I would be honored if you would join mine. And not just you, Danny. Sloane too. She's important to you, which means she's important to me as well."

He didn't trust his own instincts here, since he wanted Danny by his side any way he could get him. But Danny was right. Max's Pack loved him. Auntie Ruth was one of the prickliest, most sarcastic people he knew. Danny had called her sweet. If *she* liked Danny, then Danny was amazing. He'd do anything he could to get Danny to join them.

Neither of them were prepared when Danny's father laid a hand on each of their shoulders.

"Gentlemen, they've begun seating people," he said. He gave Max's shoulder a hard squeeze and didn't release him, apparently intent on guiding them into the ballroom.

It took all of Max's control not to growl and shrug the unwanted hand off. Touching an Alpha without permission could have ugly consequences. Max closed his eyes and took a deep breath. Was it possible Danny's father didn't know? Danny hadn't, after all. The Cresswells spent so much energy on passing for human that their senses must be dulled. Max had heard of it happening, but the stories were always about shifters who denied that part of themselves. Was that even possible for a werewolf?

Shifters didn't feel the pull of the moon like werewolves did, so he had no idea what happened on a full moon. Max imagined it was like a yearning, like when he went too long between changing and his skin ached.

"I sent your uncle an invitation to sit at our table, but his assistant declined," Mr. Cresswell said.

Max pasted on his best smile. "My uncle had another engagement tonight. He will be here to present the award, and if time allows he will mingle afterward."

Mr. Cresswell gritted his teeth. "Unacceptable. I was very clear—"

"Jesus," Danny muttered, whirling around and forcing his father to stop marching them toward the ballroom. "I appreciate your donation. It's going to do a lot of good and make a real difference for these kids. But *I'm* the one who agreed to attend all these events in exchange. Not Max, and not his uncle. Me."

"You know full well what I expected when you agreed, Daniel," his father snarled.

"I don't appreciate your tone," Max said. He rolled his shoulder, dislodging Mr. Cresswell's hand.

"I don't recall asking you if you did."

Mr. Cresswell's knuckles went white against Danny's tuxedo jacket, and Danny winced. Max reached out before he'd given it conscious thought and wrapped his hand over Danny's father's, squeezing hard enough to break several bones. Mr. Cresswell gasped and let go of Danny, and Max pulled Danny behind him before Danny could react.

Max put a hand on Mr. Cresswell's back and leaned in. Anyone passing by would assume he was giving him a hug, but Max squeezed in close enough that Mr. Cresswell gasped as his broken hand was sandwiched between them.

"I admire your son too much to make a scene, but that's the only thing keeping me from putting you on the ground." Max kept his voice calm and level. "We will continue to honor the deal Danny made with you, and that includes my uncle attending the fundraiser you're organizing for the foundation. But you don't own me, nor do you own any piece of my uncle. You are not Danny's Alpha, and he will not be taking orders from you. Do you understand?"

"How I speak to my son is none of your damn business. Do you have any idea how much power I have in this city? By the time I'm done, I'll have your badge."

Mr. Cresswell stepped back, and Max let him go, moving to Danny's side.

"Daniel, I am through putting up with you dragging our family name through the mud. I'll take back every cent of that donation unless you—"

He swallowed hard when Alpha Connoll joined them, his threat trailing off before he could complete it. His jaw dropped when Alpha Connoll tilted his neck to Max, a sign of respect and deference.

"I'd heard about your donation," Connoll said. "Well past time for it, I'd say. Danny is doing amazing work, and every dollar counts."

Danny flushed under the Alpha's praise, and Max's chest tightened in jealousy. It seemed to amuse Alpha Connoll, who smirked and put a hand on Max's shoulder.

"Ah, so that's the way of it. I see. Well done, Max. You've chosen a very strong mate. He'll be quite the helpmate in guiding your Pack."

He put another hand on Danny's shoulder, but the pose, while similar to the one Mr. Cresswell had them in earlier, was anything but threatening. Max could feel the

pride and respect the older Alpha had for Danny, and he
hoped Danny could feel it too, even after Alpha Connoll
dropped his hands and the connection was lost.

Mr. Cresswell gaped at them. "What?"

"I hope I haven't let the cat out of the bag too early,"
Alpha Connoll said, his eyes sparkling with amusement.
"Or the binturong, I should say."

Max doubted the Alpha regretted it at all. And neither
did he. He was proud to be bonding with Danny, and he
would have shouted it from the rooftops if he could. It
was too early in their relationship to be talking about it
outside the Pack, but Mr. Cresswell was family and
Connoll was Danny's Alpha. They should be happy for
him. Besides, if the bond was strong enough for Connoll
to sense it, it wasn't fledgling anymore. They might not
have been together long, but their instincts were working
on overdrive to push them toward the Alpha Mate bond.

Danny had paled a bit when Alpha Connoll
congratulated them, but he regained his color as he looked
at his father's shocked face.

"I'm joining Max's Pack," he said. He hesitated,
bowing his head when he turned toward Alpha Connoll.
"That is, sir, I plan to petition to move from the Connoll
Pack to the Torres Pack. I'm sure we're breaking all
kinds of protocol here, and I apologize."

Alpha Connoll laughed. "I'd be upset if you weren't,
Danny. I can hardly protest when true love is involved,
now can I?"

From the look on Mr. Cresswell's face, he very
much wanted to protest. But he stayed silent, his mouth
a thin, angry line.

"I wouldn't worry about the safety of your badge,"
Alpha Connoll said conversationally. "Daniel and I will be
having a chat. You're welcome to join us if you'd like?"

Max hadn't been overly worried on that account. He was more concerned about the effect this confrontation would have on Danny. He'd separated himself physically from his father a decade ago, but despite his many protests to the contrary, it was obvious that Danny's father still had the ability to hurt him emotionally.

Everyone had already gone in for dinner, so they all looked up when one of the large ballroom doors creaked open. Mrs. Cresswell was bearing down on them impressively fast, given that her shoes were hardly more appropriate than Sloane's.

Max held eye contact with her as he answered Alpha Connoll's question.

"I appreciate that, but I don't want to interfere, Alpha. I'm more concerned about the impact on Danny's foundation if he goes through with his threat to pull his donation."

Alpha Connoll turned to Danny. "The Connoll Pack would be honored to make a matching donation to the foundation, Danny. In the event that your father rescinds his support, ours will remain. Consider it a mating gift."

"He most certainly will not rescind the donation," Mrs. Cresswell said when she reached them. She looked at Danny, her expression stricken. "Daniel, I am so sorry. Alpha Connoll, please accept my apologies. I didn't hear everything, but I heard enough."

The Alpha inclined his head.

"This isn't your doing, Veronica. You have no cause to apologize."

She took Danny's father by the elbow of his injured hand, making him wince.

"Danny, please make our excuses to the table. Your father has fallen ill, and I'm afraid I need to take him home immediately."

Danny's eyes widened, and he met Max's gaze. The citrusy-sweet scent of Danny's surprised gratitude cut through the anger and fear in the hallway. It only made Max angrier—Danny shouldn't be surprised that his mother came to his aid. That was a mother's *job*. Clearly it hadn't happened much in Danny's life.

"Thank you, Mother," Danny said, his voice hoarse.

She made eye contact with Danny. "Would you mind terribly if I came by to see you tomorrow? I— there is so much I don't know about your life, and the fault is entirely mine."

Max put a hand on Danny's shoulder. He could feel him trembling, and his protective instinct welled over. He wanted to answer for Danny, but that was the last thing Danny needed right now. Max needed to show him that he wasn't just trading one controlling Alpha for another. Even though it physically hurt, he kept his mouth shut.

Danny glanced back at him and offered him a small smile. Max couldn't even imagine what he must smell like now. His struggle was probably clear to everyone, which was humiliating. It certainly wasn't fitting of an Alpha of Max's status. But if he wanted Danny as his Alpha Mate, Max was going to have to get used to feeling like this. Danny wasn't his to speak for or command.

"I have plans with the Torres Pack tomorrow," Danny said, reaching up to give Max's fingers a squeeze. "But why don't you come to the foundation office Monday morning? I can give you a tour of the offices and the day center, and then maybe we can go to lunch."

The sincerity in Danny's voice made Max's chest hurt. He hoped Mrs. Cresswell was serious about getting to know her son. Otherwise she was just setting Danny up for even more heartbreak.

"That sounds lovely."

Mr. Cresswell started to speak, but Alpha Connoll cut him off with a barely audible growl.

Both Cresswells flinched, but Mrs. Cresswell recovered first. Her expression was grim and her posture ramrod straight.

"Please enjoy the evening, Alpha Connoll," Mrs. Cresswell said. "I'm sorry you had to see our family like this."

Alpha Connoll pursed his lips. "I'm not," he said bluntly. "My only regret is I didn't see this years ago when I could have actually helped Danny."

Mrs. Cresswell kept her head held high, but tears glazed her eyes. She led Mr. Cresswell out of the lobby, leaving Max standing alone with Danny and Alpha Connoll.

"Why don't the two of you head out as well? I can explain to Sloane and the rest of your father's table," Connoll offered. He paused and shook his head with a soft laugh. "Or rather, I can tell the table both Danny and his father fell ill and went home. I'll tell Sloane the truth, of course. But the rest of the table is human."

Danny's lips curled into a sneer. "My father only associates with Supes when it will be socially or financially beneficial. He thinks of his wolf as a birth defect."

Max could barely contain his anger. Things had been worse for Danny than he realized. He regretted letting Mr. Cresswell go with a few broken bones in his hand. He should have shattered it.

"I'm sorry you were raised carrying that burden, Danny," Alpha Connoll said.

"It's no one's fault but my father's," Danny said. He leaned heavily against Max. "If you'll excuse us, Alpha, I think I need to get Max upstairs before he explodes."

Was Danny getting better at deciphering scents or was it just that obvious that Max was about to lose his shit? He'd held his instincts at bay pretty well in a stressful situation, but his control was slipping.

Alpha Connoll chuckled.

"I remember what a new bond is like," he said. "Don't let me keep you."

Danny wrapped an arm around Max's waist and headed for the elevators. Neither of them said a word until they were back in the suite.

Max huffed out a soft laugh when he saw the open bedroom door. It hadn't even been an hour since he'd been in here fantasizing about getting Danny out of his tuxedo. Now sex was the furthest thing from his mind. He had so many questions for Danny about his childhood and his relationship to his inner wolf. Did he even *want* to be with a Pack that celebrated their shifter ability? Would he feel comfortable on Pack runs and at ceremonies and rituals where everyone shifted?

"Hey," Danny said, coming up behind Max and running his hands over his shoulders. He tugged on the lapels, and Max let him slide the tuxedo coat off. "What's going on in your head?"

Chapter Nine

MAX had been tense and upset, so Danny told him to go take a shower. While he was alone, Danny ordered room service and a bottle of wine. It wouldn't take the edge off like it would for a human, but it just seemed more civilized to have a serious discussion about their future over a glass of good cabernet.

Danny changed and hung his tux in the closet. Tonight had been terrible, but there were still three more events to attend before the summer was over. He'd made a deal, and he was going to keep it. He just wished he knew if he'd be attending with Max by his side or not.

The food arrived before Max finished his shower, which was more a testament to how long he'd spent in the bathroom than it was the speed of the room service. Danny would have worried he'd hurt himself in there, but as an Alpha, Max was pretty indestructible.

At least Danny assumed he was. He didn't know much about his own kind, and he knew even less about shifters. He'd come home from Camp H.O.W.L. excited about his new abilities, and his father had locked him in the pool house for a week until he was absolutely sure Danny had full control over his shift. Since then, he'd only shifted during Pack runs during the full moon.

Danny look in a lungful of air after the porter left, challenging himself to separate out all the disparate scents in the room. He hadn't practiced this since he was nineteen. It was embarrassing. He'd let his father color how he felt about his wolf, and he'd been kept isolated enough from the Pack that he hadn't formed any real bonds with them.

He should have gotten more involved with the Pack after he'd gotten out from under his father's thumb financially, but he hadn't. He'd been busy with grad school and then with starting the foundation. But those were just excuses. Some part of him believed his father when he said their wolves were a curse. It wasn't going to be like flipping a switch—Danny was going to have to push to get past those prejudices.

The smell of their dinner was overwhelming, but Danny took another breath and worked past that, blocking out the scent of roasted meat and steamy vegetables. The porter had been wearing a musky cologne, and Danny could easily scent where he'd been in the room. He closed his eyes and tried to go deeper.

The table in the living room had been wiped down with something lemony recently. It tickled at Danny's nose, making him want to sneeze. Max's scent was dulled by the water and the soap, but he could smell the remnants of his anger and frustration. Arousal too, both his and Max's. Probably from earlier, because neither of them were in the mood now.

He kept his eyes closed and listened hard. The suite was large and well soundproofed. But he could hear the showerhead dripping in the bathroom and the quiet *shurr* of the towel as Max rubbed himself dry.

Danny opened his eyes, his hearing and sense of smell dulling a bit as he lost his focus. Stretching his senses was amazing, like he'd been in a cramped space and finally had the chance to stand and work out all the kinks.

Embracing his abilities instead of burying them felt so different. He hadn't fully appreciated how much he'd been missing by suppressing his senses all the time.

Danny was proud of himself that he anticipated the bathroom door opening before it did. The whisper of Max's bare feet along the marble floor had given him away.

Max still looked tense when he came out, looking delicious in a thin T-shirt and a pair of sweatpants. Rivulets of water from his wet hair darkened his collar. He smelled amazing, and Danny took a step forward to bury his face against Max's neck. The shower had warmed his skin, amplifying the scent of sun-warmed grass and woodsmoke. Like most Supes, Max had showered with scentless products, and Danny's pulse quickened at the raw, male smell of him.

Max made a soft noise and brought his hands up to glide along Danny's back. Danny's nose filled with the scent of his arousal. It made Danny irrationally happy to know he had that effect on him. It made him feel powerful to be able to capture his Alpha's attention so completely, especially after the emotional showdown they'd just had downstairs.

Wait. Did he just think of Max as *his* Alpha? He pulled away, startled by the track his thoughts had taken. Max eyed him carefully but didn't comment on the way Danny had stiffened and pulled away. Instead he picked up the bottle of uncorked wine and poured two glasses, handing one to Danny without a word.

Danny brought the glass to his lips, but the first sip seemed to stick in his throat. He put the glass down, busying himself with transferring the plates to the cozy table near the window. He was skittish, like he couldn't trust his own body. Was this what Max felt when he said his instincts took over? Was his inner wolf picking up on the bond and taking over?

Not that he had a problem with Max being his Alpha. He wanted to join the Torres Pack, and he was pretty sure he wanted to let the bond between them continue to strengthen until it formed the Alpha Mate union. But he wasn't used to feeling like he wasn't in control of his emotions and actions.

"We should eat before it gets cold," Danny said, even though his stomach rebelled at the thought of food.

"You don't have to serve me, you know," Max said, voice full of amusement as he watched Danny arrange their plates.

"I kind of feel like I do," Danny snapped.

Max looked at him like he'd sprouted two heads. "If this is about your father—"

"It's about my instincts screaming that I need to take care of you," Danny blurted. "I don't have a clue what I'm doing, but everything in me makes me want to make sure you're okay. You're tense, and you smell like you're on edge. It's making me feel that way too."

Max was at his side in a flash, dark eyes full of worry. He cupped Danny's face in his warm hands.

"I'm sorry, Danny. I didn't realize you were that sensitive to my emotions. I'll try to do better to shield them."

He released Danny, and Danny took a seat at the table, feeling silly for being so moody but unable to find a thread of the happiness that had been so strong a minute ago.

"I'm fine," Danny muttered. He stabbed at a green bean with his fork, not waiting for Max to eat first. It made him feel a little bit better to buck that particular tradition. He wasn't going to defer to Max, even if they ended up mated.

"You've had a rough night," Max said. He sipped his wine but didn't touch his food.

"So have you. You need to eat."

Max shook his head. "I can't. My mate is upset and I caused it. I don't—listen, the instincts are new to me too, okay? Food is the furthest thing from my mind until I make sure you're okay."

Danny put his fork down with a growl. "Is this what mating is? Because it's miserable."

Max stood up and held a hand out to Danny to pull him out of his chair and lead him across the room to the sofa. He sat and arranged Danny so he was half-in, half-out of Max's lap. It should have been awkward, his torso cradled against Max's, but it wasn't. He stomach calmed instantly and the dread that had been thrumming in his chest disappeared.

"What the fuck," he said flatly, glaring at Max.

"You accepted me as your Alpha in the lobby." Max's words were quiet, and even with his sensitive hearing Danny had to listen closely to hear them. They were barely louder than the pounding of their hearts. "I don't know if you realized what you were doing, but when you told Alpha Connoll you intended to join my Pack, something happened. My Alpha instincts reacted to the beginning of the Pack bond to you, and everything went into overdrive. It's—I already felt the mating bond. And now to have you bound to the Pack, bound to *me*, in another way, it was hard not to drag you out of there. Alpha Connoll isn't a threat. I know he isn't. But my instincts are too raw, and having him near you was physically painful."

Danny ran a hand through Max's hair. It was thick and stuck up as it dried, and Danny liked how it fell through his fingers.

"I didn't know. I'm sorry."

Max leaned forward and rested their foreheads together. "Don't be sorry. I'm the one who should apologize. I'm still adjusting to the Alpha spark. It's a lot to handle. And the mate bond on top of it.... God, Danny, sometimes I feel like I'm a cub again, unable to control my shift."

Danny wasn't sure how to respond to that, so he nestled closer and kept quiet.

"I'm terrified that I'm going to do something to fuck this up," Max admitted. "You have every right to be distrustful of Alphas. You haven't really had a good example of one in your life."

That wasn't fair to Alpha Connoll, but Danny didn't think arguing with Max would help the situation.

Danny's stomach growled, and Max had the two of them on their feet before Danny could blink.

"You need to eat," Max said, letting him go so he could sit.

"Back atcha, buddy." Danny gestured to Max's untouched food.

Max pushed mashed potatoes around his plate until Danny started eating, after which Max followed suit, though begrudgingly.

"I figured bears would have a big appetite," Danny said. "And the Alpha spark burns more calories on top of that."

"I'm not actually a bear, you know. It's the easiest way to explain on the fly, but binturongs are a bearcat."

Danny couldn't picture that, but he wasn't about to yank out his phone to Google it now that Max was finally eating. He needed to keep him talking so he'd relax.

"I was envisioning more like a grizzly. You know, standing in a stream spearing salmon with your claws."

Max laughed. "Binturongs are actually omnivores. Which means while we have to eat a lot when we shift, it doesn't have to be red meat. We eat a lot of pork and rice after our Pack runs."

"You eat a lot of pork, period. That thing we had the other night, what was it called? The fried pig. So good."

"Crispy pata," Max supplied for him. "Yeah, that's one of my favorite things. We don't have it often because it's a pain to make on that scale at home, but it usually shows up at special occasions."

"Like your grandmother coming home after spending months in the Philippines."

Max's lips quirked. "Like the Alpha bringing home a guy for the first time."

Danny couldn't help but grin at that. "Really?"

"Really. It was just supposed to be a family cookout until Tori spilled the beans about you coming, and suddenly half the Pack wanted to come."

"Where do you go for your Pack runs? There aren't any bearcats around here for you to blend in with."

Max gave him an incredulous look. "There aren't any gigantic wolves around here either. We go up north to a campground."

"Is your form big? I mean, bearcats sound small."

"Actual binturongs are smallish. They're related to civets. But we're just like you. We keep roughly the same mass when we shift, so we're much bigger than the average wild binturong."

Danny had heard of civets. His mother had imported civet coffee for a luncheon once. He and Sloane had dared each other to drink it, but they'd both chickened out.

"Do binturongs eat coffee beans?"

Max made a face. "If you're asking if binturong-poop coffee exists, no. It doesn't. It's a common question."

"Just checking," Danny said, smiling so hard his cheeks hurt.

They put the plates back on the cart, and Max wheeled it into the hallway. Danny was grateful. The smell of the food had been mouthwatering when he'd been hungry, but it was distracting now that he'd eaten his fill.

Danny caught Max in a loose embrace when he came back in. He drew him in for a kiss, soft and undemanding. Max looped his arms around Danny's back, pulling them closer together as he deepened the kiss, and Danny let him take control of it until both of them were breathing hard.

He pulled back, his throat catching at how blissed-out Max looked. He had to admit his inner wolf was feeling about the same.

"Thanks for being here with me tonight," Danny said. "And for not mauling my father earlier, even though he deserved it."

"Bringing up your father isn't doing much for the mood," Max joked.

Danny leaned their heads together. "I was thinking more about how you fought off your Alpha asshole instincts and let me handle myself," he murmured. "That was pretty hot."

Max's next chuckle sounded forced. "So all I have to do to turn you on is keep an iron grip on my instincts and let you speak and think for yourself? That's a pretty low bar."

"It's really not. You're an exceptionally good guy."

Max's shoulders were still stiff with tension, so Danny kneaded them lightly, his arousal spiking when Max's eyes fluttered shut.

"Would you let me give you a massage? To help you relax, I mean."

Max opened his eyes. "I don't think I'd find that particularly relaxing."

"I'm pretty good at it. I took a kinesiology class in undergrad, and we had to learn how muscle groups work together. There was an extra credit project on massage—"

"That's not what I meant," Max said. Danny was thankful he'd cut off his rambling. He tended to do that when he was nervous, and kissing Max definitely made him nervous. He pressed a light kiss to Danny's mouth. "While having your hands all over me definitely sounds like fun, I think it would be counterproductive if your goal is for me to relax."

That sounded like a challenge, and Danny never backed down from one of those. He grinned and hooked a finger in the waistband of Max's sweats, pulling him toward the bedroom. Max followed without further protest.

"This is, what, our fifth date? Sixth? I think it might be time to pull the plug on going slow. We both agreed this isn't casual."

Max cupped a hand over Danny's cheek and gave him another soft, slow kiss.

"While I would love to do that, and trust me, I would *love* to do that, I'm not sure it's a good idea to make that decision when we're both emotionally wrung out and exhausted," he said. "This isn't taking it to the next level physically, it's consummating the bond."

Danny hated to admit it, but Max was right. He was sure he'd still want to have sex with Max tomorrow, but it was a good idea to wait until they'd both had some time to process what happened tonight.

"I like morning sex better anyway," Danny teased, laughing out loud when the steady thrum of Max's pulse quickened.

He was really enjoying reconnecting with his senses. And he had a feeling it was going to make sex much more intense. That was definitely worth waiting for, especially since the wait was only going to be a few hours if he had anything to say about it.

They shared the bathroom sink as they got ready for bed, and it was more intimate than anything Danny had ever done. Max looked rumpled and sleepy, and the way he rubbed at his eyes as he fought off sleep while they sat up in bed talking was almost irresistibly adorable.

Danny let Max curl around him when they turned off the light. He'd never been comfortable enough to just drift right off to sleep with someone else in his bed, but lying there with Max didn't feel awkward or uncomfortable. Danny listened to Max's even breathing until it put him to sleep.

IT wasn't unusual for Danny to wake up with his covers tangled around him. He was a restless sleeper, and he had a hard time falling asleep and staying asleep. So he was surprised to find he and Max had barely moved at all when he woke the next morning.

They had plans to meet Sloane for breakfast, but it couldn't be much past six, judging from the light streaming in the window. They hadn't bothered to pull the shades when they'd gone to bed last night, and Danny was glad. Max's skin looked perfect in the soft glow of the weak sunlight. Danny gave in to temptation and let his fingers trail lightly over Max's exposed shoulder. Max twitched and opened his eyes, a sleepy smile curving his lips when he realized Danny was looking at him.

"Morning." Max wiggled an arm out of the duvet and used it to pull Danny closer so he was lying on Max's chest. The thin T-shirt he'd slept in had ridden up in his sleep, and Danny splayed his hand over the bare skin, fascinated by the way the muscles contracted under his touch.

"Ah, Danny," Max bit out when Danny continued his exploration. "That's… ah."

Danny laughed and let his fingers dip farther, tracing the outline of Max's morning erection, which presented an oh-so-tempting bulge in his sweatpants. Max told him they'd reevaluate in the morning, and it was morning. Danny wasn't going to be held back anymore, not unless this really wasn't what Max wanted. And from the way the bulge jumped when Danny's fingers traced lightly over it, he didn't think that was the case.

"I've had a good night's sleep," Danny said before Max could speak. "The best night's sleep, actually. I slept like a rock. I still want to join your Pack. I still want to get to know you and continue this bond, and I'm not scared that the end of that line is taking my place as the Alpha Mate in your Pack, assuming things go well. Have I addressed all your objections?"

He laid his palm over the bulge and squeezed lightly. Max shuddered and groaned, his hips bucking up, trying to follow when Danny took his hand away.

"I'm of sound mind and very sound body," Danny continued, pressing his own flannel-covered erection against Max's hip. "And I know exactly what I'm offering."

Max grunted and hauled Danny up for a kiss.

"I don't know that I'm in sound mind," he said, his voice rough. "Not after waking up to that. God, Danny. You don't have any idea how much I want you."

Danny smirked and bared his throat. He didn't have to look to know Max would be fixated on it. The resulting growl was very satisfying, as was the way Max lunged forward and latched on to the exposed skin. Danny wished he could carry the mark like a human would, a hickey that would have lasted for days if not for Danny's healing factor.

He could smell how much Max wanted him. The bedroom was thick with arousal and excitement, his own scent mingling with Max's to form something that smelled so good Danny wanted to bottle it and take it with him everywhere. Was this the mate bond flaring up as it solidified, or would it always be like this?

He could feel Max's desperation through their bond. It was wilder than his, and that sent a thrill through Danny. Max was so much more in tune with his shifter side than Danny. He didn't know if that was responsible for the almost feral tint to the feelings or if it was Max's Alpha side driving it. Either way, it was the hottest thing Danny had ever experienced. It was like a feedback loop—Max's arousal fed into Danny's, pushing both of them higher and higher until Danny wanted Max with a fierceness that was almost painful.

Max kneaded his way down Danny's back until his clever fingers reached Danny's ass. Danny lost his breath when Max's strong hands cupped his ass, a moan punching out of him when Max used his thumbs to push the fabric down so his palms could rest on Danny's bare skin.

His touch was electric, setting Danny's skin on fire. His cock throbbed, confined by the flannel sleep pants. He pushed against Max's hip, desperate for more friction, more pressure, more *anything*.

Max chuckled, the sound reverberating through Danny's entire body. He tugged on the sleep pants again, and Danny lifted his hips, letting Max free his cock from its flannel cage. Danny's entire body went taut when Max closed a warm hand around his erection, giving it a teasing pump that made Danny arch and writhe.

Max released him, and Danny fought to silence the whimper in his throat. Max didn't leave him hanging for long. He kissed the column of Danny's throat and slid down Danny's body until he could rub his face against Danny's exposed hip. His stubble was rough against Danny's oversensitive skin, and he fisted his hands in the blanket to stop himself from grabbing Max's head to reposition it a little bit lower. Max was being an agonizing tease, and Danny was torn between loving the way his entire body was singing with anticipation and hating it.

He tried to spread his legs to make room for Max, but his pajama pants were tangled around his thighs. Max sat back and helped free him, then urged Danny up so he could take Danny's shirt off too.

Being naked while Max was fully clothed made Danny's already racing pulse speed up. He wanted to see Max naked more than anything, but he also liked the way Max was so fixated on his body that he couldn't even take the time to rip his own clothes off. Danny's wolf wanted to preen at the attention his Alpha was giving him.

Something must have changed subtly in his scent, because Max inhaled deeply and his eyes flashed gold.

"Fuck. You look so good spread out for me," Max murmured. He settled between Danny's legs and lowered his head, nosing against Danny's balls. "I'm going to take care of you. Make it so good for you that you can't even look at another guy."

He licked a stripe up Danny's dick, laughing when Danny nearly jumped out of his skin. Max planted a hand on either side of Danny's hips and took him in his mouth. Wet heat engulfed him tip to root, and Danny couldn't get enough air. He sucked in a greedy lungful, panting as Max's mouth moved over him. This was going to be over embarrassingly fast if he didn't do something to slow Max down.

Danny let go of the blanket and ran a hand through Max's hair. The wild strands were silky and thick, and Danny brushed them back from Max's face and stroked a thumb over Max's forehead to get his attention.

Max looked up, eyes glinting, and swiped his tongue over the head of Danny's cock.

Danny arched up off the bed, his fingers tightening in Max's hair as he let out a string of curses.

"Max, c'mon," he rasped. "I want to get a taste of you too."

Max released him and scrambled up, ripping at his clothes as he moved. *Thank God*, Danny thought. A minute longer and he'd have come down Max's throat. He didn't want their first time to be over that quickly.

Max's chest was as defined as his stomach. Danny traced a finger down Max's side, grinning when Max shivered and broke into gooseflesh.

"I offered you a massage last night," Danny said, coming up on his knees. "How about I follow through on that now? You look tense, Alpha."

Max's eyes went glassy when Danny addressed him as Alpha. He didn't know why he'd done it, but he liked the result. It clearly turned Max on to be addressed like that, and it gave Danny a thrill that he could have that effect on him with something so small.

He waited for Max to arrange himself facedown on the bed, which ended up involving several pillows. Danny smirked, pleased that Max was aroused enough he couldn't quite get comfortable.

Danny straddled Max's upper thighs, enjoying the way Max let out a breathy moan when Danny's dick bobbed and rubbed along his ass as Danny leaned down to knead at the tense muscles in Max's upper back.

He'd chosen this position to see how his Alpha would react to being in a more submissive pose. The musky rich smell of his arousal hadn't flagged a bit, even when Danny's cock smeared precome along his cheeks as Danny stretched to massage his shoulders.

Danny worked his way down Max's back, intent on kneading all the stress out of him, even though each touch built up more tension in Danny. He used his thumbs to work down Max's spine until he was rubbing circles at the base of it, his fingers teasing down the swell of Max's ass. Max's breath caught every time he did it, and before long his hips were squirming. The motion pressed Max's ass against Danny's erection, and both of them dragged in a harsh breath.

Danny used the heels of his hands to push up Max's back, following the stiff massage by lying on top of Max, his chest covering the smooth expanse of Max's back.

"Want to flip over so I can do your front?" Danny whispered in his ear.

Max had them flipped before Danny could register he was moving. He pinned Danny to the bed, trapping the hands Danny had been teasing him with against the pillow. His face was flushed, and his heart was beating so hard Danny was half-convinced he could see it fluttering at Max's throat.

"I want to finish what I started," Max murmured.

He let go of Danny so he could wrap his hand around both of their cocks. Danny worked his freed hands down between them so he could help. He locked a hand around Max's and kept pace with his strokes. It was too dry and a little awkward, but that didn't stop it from feeling amazing. Danny's muscles were screaming like he'd been on edge forever, even though it couldn't have been more than an hour; probably less. Time seemed to stop when he was caught up in Max. He'd never experienced anything like it.

His orgasm built quickly, and it didn't take more than a half-dozen strokes before he spilled over their wrists. Max's nostrils flared at the scent, and he groaned, following Danny over seconds later.

Danny had written simultaneous orgasms off as a fairy tale, but apparently not. Or maybe they were just so in tune through the bond that his orgasm overstimulated Max. He'd like to test the theory some time. Maybe even yet this morning.

Good to know that even awesome sex wasn't enough to turn off the running commentary in his head. Danny laughed at himself, shaking his head when Max quirked an eyebrow at him.

"It's nothing. I mean, this wasn't nothing. This was the best orgasm I've had in forever. But I was thinking about the bond and all the things I want to do to you to test it out."

"Is that so?" Max rolled off him, padded to the bathroom, and returned with a towel for each of them.

Danny cleaned himself up as best he could. "My undergraduate degree is in sociology. What kind of social scientist would I be if I didn't carefully examine all aspects of this bond?"

"For science," Max said, amused.

"And because it's fun," Danny admitted. He sighed when his alarm went off. "We're supposed to meet Sloane for breakfast in half an hour."

Max got out of bed again, and Danny lost his train of thought as the muscles in Max's back rippled as he moved. They were mesmerizing.

"Think she'll have Oscar with her?"

"Sloane? Probably. She's so focused on finishing medical school at the top of her class. When she does go out, she tends to live it up."

He loved the way Max moved, all confidence and animal grace. Watched as he walked across the room, completely comfortable with himself and his nudity. If Danny looked like that, he'd want to be naked all the time.

Max held out a hand. "Want to shower together?"

"Will we actually shower if we do that?"

Max grinned. "Only one way to find out."

OSCAR was indeed sitting with Sloane in the hotel restaurant when they made their way downstairs. They were only fifteen minutes late, which Danny thought was some sort of miracle. They'd spent most of their time in the shower fooling around, but somehow both of them managed to get clean and be dressed and downstairs before Sloane came after them.

Max stooped to give Sloane a kiss on the cheek and punched Oscar lightly in the shoulder when he stood to greet them. He was wearing his tuxedo shirt and pants, but he'd ditched the bow tie and jacket. It very much looked like a walk-of-shame breakfast, but Oscar didn't seem bothered in the least. If anything, he looked proud to be sitting there in last night's clothes.

"Oscar said he and Max had an appointment this morning, so we went ahead and ordered for you," Sloane said when they'd taken their seats.

That was the first Danny had heard of it. Max and Oscar had a brief but animated conversation, keeping their voices low. Danny did his best to tune out to give them privacy. Max sat back with a sigh and put his arm around the back of Danny's chair. It was casual but calculated, and it made Danny's pulse skip. He normally hated possessive behavior, but this felt natural and not like a declaration of ownership.

"There was a murder overnight. Detectives on the case think it might be connected to our investigation, so we've got to go talk with them. Sorry, Danny," he said, brushing his fingers over Danny's back lightly. "I'd hoped we could spend the day together."

Danny wished they had more time, but he had some investigating to do himself today. Sloane's private detective had a lead for him, and Danny was meeting with her after lunch to get the information. It had been weeks since anyone had seen Joss, and Danny was getting increasingly worried.

"It's okay. I kind of like that your job involves crazy hours. It means you won't be upset when I'm the one cancelling dates because I have an emergency appearance in court or I have to go calm a foster family down after their charge has blown something up or something."

Sloane looked between the two of them, beaming. "Does this mean you had the DTR conversation?"

Danny snorted. He assumed her comment was for Oscar's benefit, because she was well aware of the mate bond he and Max shared. Their relationship had been defined from the moment they met—they had just been slow to catch up.

Max fluttered his eyelashes and reached for Danny's hand. "Yes, Sloane. We went out for milkshakes last night, and I gave Danny my pin. We're officially going steady now."

"Oh, I bet you gave it to him last night," Sloane teased. "He has the look of someone who's been well pinned."

Danny almost choked on his orange juice. Max patted him on the back, smirking.

"Sloane!" he chastised when he could talk again. "Mind your own business. Jesus."

Sloane's grin didn't quite reach her eyes, and Danny wished he could pull her aside and ask what was wrong. She liked Max, and she'd been the one to talk him through his worries about Max's Alpha status earlier in the week. She'd curled into herself a bit, making her look even smaller in the sweatshirt she wore. It had been Danny's a year ago, but she'd stolen it after he'd moved out of the house.

Of course. She was worried about being left behind.

Max's fingers stroked against his collar, and Danny looked over. Max furrowed his brows, silently questioning Danny's sudden downturn in mood, but Danny shook his head. This wasn't the time or the place. Oscar was sitting right there, and even if he hadn't been, it wasn't his place to bring up the Pack. Besides, the invitation had to come from Max. Sloane might be too proud to accept if anyone other than Max made the offer, so Danny didn't want to risk it. He couldn't imagine being in a Pack that didn't include Sloane.

"Aunt Veronica asked if I could join her when she meets you for lunch Monday," Sloane said, changing the subject smoothly. "Operative word there being *asked*. She didn't order me to come. She wasn't slurring her speech, but for a moment I was tempted to run through the aneurysm checklist with her."

Danny laughed. "No, I can go one better. She called me Danny last night."

"More than once," Max added.

Sloane's jaw dropped. "No fucking way."

Oscar looked confused, his eyes narrowed as he studied them. "But your name *is* Danny."

Sloane made a strangled noise that was between a laugh and a hiccup. "His name is Daniel Alexander Cresswell the fourth," she corrected. "And the first time someone called him Danny, Aunt Veronica pitched a fit."

"And fired him," Danny said. "It was my tennis instructor. I was nine. She fired him on the spot."

Oscar's eyebrows rose. "No shit? For what? Calling a kid by a socially acceptable nickname isn't usually grounds for dismissal."

"She's fired people for less," Sloane muttered.

"God, I don't even remember," Danny said. He ran a hand through his hair, trying to picture the instructor. He'd been a college kid, he recalled that much. Now that he really thought about it, he'd had a huge crush on the guy. That might have had more to do with his firing than anything.

But he'd loved being called Danny, whether it was because a cute older guy had been the first one to do it or because it was something that was *his*, he wasn't sure. But it had stuck.

And his mother using it meant more to him than he could explain. She seemed to be realizing he was his own person, and more importantly, she was trying to accept that. It was a miracle.

He probably had Max to thank for her change of heart, but it didn't matter. She was trying, and that was all that mattered.

Danny's stomach growled when the food arrived. Max gave him a suggestive little wink that made Danny's stomach swoop—he knew exactly why he was so hungry. He and Max had worked up an appetite this morning, and he'd been too emotional to do much more than pick at the dinner room service had brought last night.

"I gotta say, you seem pretty normal for someone who grew up that rich," Oscar said as Danny dug into the waffle Sloane had ordered him.

He caught Max's eye at just the right time, and both of them broke into giggles. Sloane joined in a second later, coughing as she swallowed her bite of egg.

"Normal," Danny repeated, still laughing. "I guess."

"Hey, money aside, you're as normal as I am," Max said, setting Sloane off into a fresh peal of laughter.

Oscar shook his head and kept eating. "I take it back. None of you are normal."

Max bumped Danny's knee under the table, leaving his leg there as a warm, comforting presence. It helped Danny get control of himself. It hadn't been *that* funny, but he was feeling a little on edge. It wasn't going to take much to push him off into hysterical laughter or a torrent of tears. Everything was changing so quickly. Even things he'd always been able to count on, like his mother's judgmental attitude, were changing.

"Did we miss much last night?" Danny asked.

Sloane rolled her eyes. "So boring. I'm jealous you got out of it."

"Your uncle's friend was cool," Oscar said. "The big one. The others not so much."

"Al—uh, Mr. Connoll is a family friend," Sloane said. Danny kicked her under the table. "We also sat with Uncle Daniel's newest business partner and his wife. They were dull, dull, dull."

"When he found out I was a cop, all he wanted to talk about were zoning ordinances," Oscar said. "He has some building that's on hold because the neighborhood kicked up a fuss and had a protest when he tried to break ground. He wanted to know if I could go arrest them."

"He literally talked about it all night," Sloane said in disgust.

"But Mr. Connoll, he was an all-right guy. Real interesting for a stuffed shirt."

Danny choked on his orange juice again. He couldn't imagine anyone calling Alpha Connoll a stuffed shirt. He radiated power. Did humans really not feel it?

Max finished his coffee and looked at his watch. "What time did you say we needed to be there?"

Oscar groaned. "Soon."

He pulled his wallet out of his pocket, but Sloane waved him off. "I'll charge it to the room," she said.

"I had a lot of fun. We should do it again sometime," Oscar said.

Sloane let him lean in and kiss her on the cheek, but Danny doubted there would be a next time. That wasn't her style.

"I'll call you when I'm done," Max said, giving Danny a quick kiss. "We can go by the house if you want. See who's around to bug."

Spending the afternoon at Max's parents' house sounded wonderful, but Danny had things to do.

"I've got a thing in the afternoon, but maybe for dinner?"

"One taste and you're addicted to Pinoy," Max teased.

Danny grinned at the double entendre, laughing when Max caught up a second later and grimaced.

"Keep it family friendly, Torres," Oscar said. He clapped Danny on the shoulder. "See you later, Danny. I've got to take your man to work."

Sloane leaned in as soon as they left the table. "So—"

Danny shook his head. He didn't want Max to know he'd hired a private investigator.

He waited until he couldn't hear Max's heartbeat even when he strained for it before talking.

"I'm meeting her today. She thinks she's found Joss. If it's him, he's been living behind a Dumpster, so he doesn't have the stuff with him."

"He probably sold it that night. I don't think there's any chance of you getting those gifts back, Danny."

"I've already replaced everything. I don't care about the gifts—I want to make sure Joss is okay. He's a good kid, Sloane. He wouldn't have taken that stuff unless he had to."

She gave him a skeptical look. "Had to?"

"Look, you don't know what it's like for these kids. He could have fallen in with a gang and been forced to do it for initiation. Or"—he leaned in closer, whispering—"he could have been forced by a witch or something. I know him. He's had a hard life, but he isn't a criminal."

"Except that he is, if your hunch that he broke into your apartment is right," Sloane said. "You're too trusting, Danny."

He knew he was. But he had to be. The kids he worked with were skittish and often dangerous. And most of them could scent a lie at fifty paces. They were good kids who'd been put in terrible situations. They had no reason to trust him, which is why he had to trust *them*. He had to be the one to bend because they couldn't.

"Do you want me to come with you?"

He wasn't going to drag Sloane into this. Not that she couldn't take care of herself—she could. But she'd stick out like a sore thumb, and he needed to blend in if he had any hope of finding Joss and actually getting to talk to him.

"Thanks, but this isn't really your thing."

She blew out a breath. "Thank God. I'm going to be spending the day at the library. Text if you need me? And it better not be for bail."

He laughed. "I'd call Max if I needed bail. Maybe he'd get a discount."

Her smile was practically feral. "So that's progressing, then."

Danny shook his head. "Don't be nosy."

"I don't have to be nosy to know you two fucked," she said, wrinkling her nose. "You both reek. But you smell happy, so I'll deal."

He was. Danny wasn't sure he'd ever been this happy, actually. But he wasn't going to give Sloane any more information than necessary. She was a terrible gossip, and things were too new with Max to share with the world. He wanted to have him to himself for a little while longer.

"Are you heading straight to meet the investigator?"

The waitress brought over the bill, and he signed it to his room and left her a hefty tip since they'd probably caused a scene with all their laughing.

"I have barely enough time to swing by home and change," he said. "Are you ready to check out, or are you spending the rest of the morning here?"

"I booked a massage," she said. "I usually do the morning after a social event with Uncle Daniel."

Danny should probably stop by and check on his parents, but that could take hours. Last night had been awful, and he was sure they'd be dealing with the fallout from it for weeks, if not months, to come. But they were adults; they could take care of themselves.

They'd keep, but Joss might not.

Chapter Ten

AS the days passed and more and more robberies piled up, Max's frustration at not being able to clue his partner in to the supernatural currents grew. They'd been called in to meet with the port authority this afternoon after a random sweep turned up a shipping container of stolen goods linked to Max and Oscar's case. It was the best lead they'd had in the case, but it still didn't tell them who was behind the theft ring or how they were picking their targets.

"At least we know where they're going now," Oscar said as they walked out of the precinct. "That's more of the puzzle than we had this morning."

The electronics had been found in a shipping container bound for Guangzhou that was registered as an empty shipment. The agent told them there had been an increase in empty containers heading back to China since the demand for scrap metal and other junk to mine for recyclable material had shifted from China to India.

Oscar was unfailingly optimistic. Max had sat through the same meeting, and he had no idea how Oscar could think they were any better off. If anything, finding the shipping container was derailing their investigation.

"Who knows, we might be able to tie this up tonight. You ready for a good old-fashioned stakeout?"

No, he really wasn't. Six hours in a van with Oscar's beef-jerky farts was enough to try the resolve of any man. Besides, there was zero chance whoever filled that shipping container was returning for it. The port authority had left it where it was in the hopes the thieves would be back with more goods to finish filling it, but Max knew better.

Customs and Border Protection might have been discreet in its investigation, but agents had entered the shipping container. When Max and Oscar had visited the scene in plain clothes, he'd known the shipping container would be a dead end.

It had reeked of ozone, the telltale smell of heavy magic. He'd bet his detective shield that the thing had been warded to the gills. The witch would have known the moment CBP touched it.

At least it had confirmed his suspicion that there were Supes involved. One witch couldn't have set wards that strong. Not without help.

Oscar had been glued to his side since the task-force meeting, so he hadn't had a chance to call Jackson to get his take on things. With both of them working the Supe angle, they'd turn something up sooner or later, but Max didn't have time to waste. The first death had opened a seal of sorts—the ring was getting more violent and less cautious, which was not a good thing. They'd taken two more victims, security guards at a warehouse that had been hit yesterday. Homicide was chomping at the bit to take over the investigation completely, and Max was running out of reasons to stop them.

Small crimes were surging too. Burglaries like Danny's had increased 60 percent, and tourists were getting mugged for their cell phones left and right. Something had to be done, and soon.

"The shipyard is loaded with cameras, and these guys managed to get that shipping container half-filled without being caught on any of them. What makes you think we'll be any more successful?"

Oscar pulled away from the curb, snaking out into traffic with barely a glance in his mirrors. Driving with Oscar always gave Max heartburn. At least he knew he'd heal if Oscar crashed—he shuddered to think what Oscar's human partners had thought of his driving.

"You, buddy. I've never worked with anyone who is as freakishly good at sniffing someone out as you are."

Max sent him a sideways glance, but Oscar was staring straight ahead. He'd been with Oscar since his promotion, and he'd been ridiculously careful not to out himself as a Supe. He scented the air surreptitiously. Oscar didn't smell scared or wary. It must have been a figure of speech.

"Eh, I'm fresher than you," Max teased. "I'm still trying to prove I deserve my shield."

Oscar was five years older and had made detective a year and a half ago. It was a tired joke between them, but Oscar laughed anyway.

"I heard about you when you were on patrol, you know," Oscar said. "That deli robbery? Everyone on the force talked about that one."

Max had been off duty when he'd heard gunshots six blocks away. He'd made it to the deli before the asshole had even cleared out the till. He hadn't given it a second thought—he'd charged in wearing a T-shirt and running shorts and had the guy on the ground in ten seconds flat.

He'd been new to the job, right out of the academy. It probably would have been fine, but a columnist for the *New York Post* had been in the deli. Max had made the front page, and he'd taken an ungodly amount of ribbing for it. He'd also gotten an earful from his Alpha about toning down his abilities and not charging into situations like that unarmed.

Supes flew under the radar, and front-page news stories about their bravery weren't exactly subtle.

"Yeah," Max said, rubbing his neck as he looked out the window. "I was a bit of a hothead back then. Thought I was bulletproof. I got lucky."

He'd been shot in the shoulder last year, but he'd played it off. It had been a through and through, but he'd refused medical treatment on the scene and told his CO he'd been wearing a vest. He hadn't because they weren't standard uniform gear, but after that he'd purchased a thin Kevlar vest with his own money. He'd worn it religiously until his promotion. It would take a hell of a shot to kill him, but explaining away disappearing bullet holes was a nightmare he didn't need.

"We could use some of that luck on this case," Oscar grumbled. "If it escalates any further, those dickbags from homicide are going to take it over. Heard Stephens talking about it in the breakroom."

Homicide was *already* involved. This thing had grown far beyond the two of them. They were lucky to still have a seat at the task-force table. But Max kept his mouth shut. Oscar smelled like jealousy every time he bitched about homicide. Max didn't want to touch that with a ten-foot pole.

"You want burritos for dinner?"

Max grimaced. They were close to his favorite burrito joint, but he didn't love being cooped up with Oscar for hours after eating there. The stakeout was already going to be a long, painful exercise in futility. He didn't want to eat anywhere that would make it worse.

"Thai?" Oscar suggested, correctly reading Max's silence as disagreement. "Or that kebab cart?"

Traffic was heavy, which meant they didn't have time to stop and eat in anywhere. Whatever they got would be eaten in the van at the shipyard, and Max would be trapped with the scent of their empty containers for hours.

"How about that sandwich place by my apartment?"

They'd be heading right by it on the way. It was easy, they already knew both their orders, and it wouldn't stink up the van too badly as long as Oscar didn't order pastrami.

"Oh, I see," Oscar said with a snort. "You want an excuse to stop and say hello to lover boy."

He wouldn't say no to seeing Danny. It hadn't been that long since he'd seen him last, but he missed him like a physical ache. They'd been careful, sticking to blow jobs and hand jobs so things didn't get out of control. Max didn't want to give Danny the Alpha Mate bite accidentally. It would happen in the heat of the moment, sure, but he wanted to have Danny's full consent before they took that step.

They'd been spending nights together, alternating between his place and Danny's. He'd been skeptical of Danny's bed, given the shambles the rest of his furniture was in, but Danny had splurged on a mattress that was much nicer than Max's. Fooling around on a memory-foam mattress had been a learning experience, but luckily he and Danny didn't mind putting in enough practice to perfect it.

"It didn't even cross my mind," Max said airily.

"Sure it didn't, buddy."

"ARE you sure it's okay for me to be here?"

Max looped an arm around Danny's shoulder. "It's a birthday party, Danny, not a top secret arms summit."

This was the first afternoon they'd both had off in a week, and Max wanted them to spend it together. His nephew probably wouldn't even notice he'd brought a date, and if he did, it wasn't like Anthony would care.

His sisters were a different matter. Max tightened his arm around Danny's shoulders when Tori let out a squeal inside and rushed to the door.

"It's so good to see you!" she said, elbowing Max out of the way so she could hug Danny. "Come inside! You met Kathleen and the kids at the Pack cookout, but Phil had to work. Let me take you out back and introduce you."

Max stepped inside after them, shaking his head. "A fine greeting for your Alpha," he muttered.

"Welcome, Oh Mighty Alpha," she called in a singsong voice as she and Danny walked through the kitchen. "Thanks for bringing him!"

He dropped Anthony's present—he didn't even know what it was; Danny had picked it out—on the stack of gifts and wandered into the kitchen to grab a beer. His father was shucking corn into a trash can and watching the Mets lose badly at home.

"Can you believe this?" he asked, pointing toward the iPad with an ear of corn.

Max rubbed his cheek against his father's, scenting him. "To be honest, I can't believe Ma let you bring that to watch the game."

His father sent a shifty look at the backyard. "Let me give you some advice now that you've found a mate, son," he said. "It's always best to act first and ask forgiveness later."

Max thumped him on the back. "There's a reason the couch carried your smell more than your bedroom did when I was a kid."

"It's called a strategic retreat!" his father called after him as Max took his beer outside. "That's my second piece of mating advice for you!"

Tori was hanging off Danny's back when Max made his way over to them. Danny didn't seem bothered, so he shrugged and handed him a beer. Phil was in the middle of a story that, if memory served, Max didn't come out looking great in, and Ray and Eileen were eavesdropping from the other side of the yard, adding commentary when they thought Phil wasn't telling the story right.

There were human kids running around in the sprinkler, friends of Anthony's from school and baseball. He'd have to yell at Eileen and Ray later. Though to anyone else it would look like they were having a quiet conversation by themselves. Still, they weren't setting a great example for the kids.

No one other than family was here from the Pack. Partly because they'd be having another party for Anthony next week at the monthly Pack gathering, and partly because the young kids wouldn't be able to handle the excitement without a few slips. Until age four or five, the kids in the Pack shifted back and forth fluidly, mostly based on instinct as they learned how to navigate the world both on four paws and two feet. Kind of like how bilingual children switched between their two primary languages when they spoke, mixing up the vocabulary. It was adorable, but it also wasn't something you wanted to happen on a crowded street or at a twelve-year-old's birthday party.

Max didn't interject anything, letting his siblings tell their story. He was content to be there with them, even when Danny laughed so hard he dropped Tori.

"It sounds like you were a handful when you were a cub," Danny said after Max had helped Tori up. "I bet all of you were terrible. Your poor mother."

"Ma's a saint," Phil said. "You'll understand when you have cubs of your own. Danny, you have no idea what you and Max are in for. Kids are the worst."

Max hadn't fully digested his words before Danny's heart went nuts, loud even in the noisy backyard. He looked over, alarmed, before he caught drift of Danny's scent. It was similar to the smell of Oscar's jealousy, but lighter. Barely there, like a whisper of a thought. If he had to catalog it, Max would call it yearning, mixed with an intense smell of sadness.

Did Danny think Max didn't want cubs? That couldn't be further from the truth.

"We haven't exactly talked about cubs yet," Max said dryly, trying to deflect their attention from the hot blush on Danny's cheeks. "Let's not chase away my Alpha Mate before we finish the bond, hmm?"

He didn't think that was a big risk. Not if he'd interpreted Danny's scent right. They'd only known each other a few weeks, but it was easy to imagine having cubs with Danny. They hadn't had a serious discussion about what their future would look like if they accepted the Alpha Mate bond, but he was relieved to know Danny wanted cubs too.

Kathleen came out of the house a moment later with an enormous cake. She put it on the table and quietly asked for help getting the guests up to the deck so they could sing to Anthony. Phil took off for the sprinklers and Tori went to help her light the candles, leaving Max and Danny alone in the yard.

Danny leaned forward and buried his face against Max's T-shirt. "Sorry," he mumbled.

Max stroked the back of his head. "Nothing to be sorry for. I'm glad you want kids."

"I've always planned to adopt a Supe kid. There are so many who need a family," Danny said, his voice still muffled by the fabric. "But you'll need an heir. Someone to pass the Alpha spark to. So our kids will have to be shifters."

Max nudged Danny until he looked up at him. "I'd love to adopt, and I don't care if our kids are shifters or not. It doesn't matter."

"Phil said cubs—"

"That's just kind of a Pack default word for kid." Max brushed Danny's hair out of his face. "I don't need a biological child. We're decades out from me choosing a successor. I'm sure my nieces and nephews will have plenty of children. Our next Alpha needs to be a binturong shifter, but I'll have a whole Pack to pick from."

Danny's smile was electric, and Max couldn't help but grin back. They hurried over to the throng near the deck when the singing started, and by the time a thoroughly embarrassed Anthony had blown out his candles, Danny's scent was back to normal, no yearning or sadness to be found.

They ate cake and played games until the kids started to disperse a few hours later, leaving in little clumps until the only people left in the backyard were family.

"You have a good birthday, my man?" Max asked Anthony as they picked up paper plates and cups.

"It was okay."

Max put down the bag he'd been holding open so Anthony could throw trash into it. "Just okay?"

"Liza said she was coming, but she never showed up," Anthony said.

Max panicked. He loved his nieces and nephews and all the kids in the Pack, but he was shit at giving them advice.

"And Liza is a friend? A girlfriend? A mortal enemy?" he asked, trying and failing to get Anthony to smile.

"Liza is clearly a crush," Danny said, stepping up beside Anthony. He sat on the stairs and Anthony sank down next to him.

"Duh, Uncle Max," Anthony said, rolling his eyes.

"Yeah, duh, Uncle Max," Danny parroted, winking at Max. "Why don't you finish cleaning up while I talk to Anthony about the lovely Liza?"

Max took the life raft Danny was offering, hurrying off to give them the illusion privacy. He kept an ear on them as they talked about Anthony's crush and analyzed the last conversation he'd had with her to figure out why she hadn't come. Anthony was sure it was because she found out he liked her and hated him. Max had always thought of Anthony as a kid with unflappable confidence, but all his insecurities came pouring out as Danny gently probed.

Max had never heard Anthony say more than two or three words to an adult who wasn't Pack, but here he was pouring his heart out to a complete stranger. His mate bond with Danny was still forming. It definitely wouldn't be strong enough for the Pack to feel connected to Danny through it.

Anthony was smiling again by the time he and Danny were done talking. The kid was practically beaming, happier than Max had seen him in the last year.

"You're like the preteen whisperer. How did you do that?"

"Talking to kids who are struggling and helping them brainstorm solutions is literally my job, Max."

"Troubled kids," Max said, watching Anthony go in the house. He gave Phil a big hug, then moved on to Kathleen.

"All preteens are troubled," Danny said. "Some more than others. Puberty is hard. Their hormones are going crazy, and they feel split between being a kid and being an adult. Add in Supe stuff and yeah, there's going to be things to work through. Just because a kid comes from a loving family doesn't mean they don't have problems. Granted, not on the scale that the kids the Janus Foundation helps, but their feelings are still valid."

"You sound like a therapist."

Danny scoffed. "I'm a licensed LCSW. I *am* a therapist. I've gotten away from one-on-one therapy as the foundation has taken off and I've gotten busier, but I do still provide counseling on a case-by-case basis, usually family therapy when kids are having a hard time settling in with a foster family because they don't know how to communicate their needs in a way that is human-friendly. Plus I lead group sessions for the kids twice a week at the day center."

God, no wonder Danny was always so busy. Max knew the basic story about what the foundation did and how it came to be, but he wanted to know more, both about Danny and the organization he'd created to help Supe kids.

"I've been meaning to ask you where the foundation got its name," he said.

"Janus is the Greek god of new beginnings and transitions. That's what we hope to give these kids. Plus he's usually depicted with two faces because he's always looking into the past and into the future. I liked the symbolism for Supes. We all have to wear two faces, whether we physically shift or not. These kids have had to learn how to act human in order to survive, and the Janus Foundation helps them get back a piece of their other side."

Max reached out and wrapped a hand around Danny's neck, urging him in closer until their lips met. It was a soft, sweet kiss, but Max hoped it told Danny just how incredible he was. He was the most compassionate person Max knew.

"It's the perfect name," Max said when he stepped back. "Thanks for talking to Anthony. Whatever you said to him really seemed to help."

Danny grinned. "That's the best part—I didn't say anything to him. I don't have all the answers. Hell, I don't even know all the questions. Anthony helped himself. He just needed someone to listen."

Max didn't believe that for a second. Anthony needed the right person to listen, and that person was Danny. The Pack was so lucky to have him, and in a few weeks it would be official. Tonight they'd run with the Connoll Pack to celebrate Danny's last full moon with them. They needed to leave soon if they were going to be settled in by moonrise.

"We've got to get on the road," Max said when they popped into the kitchen to say goodbye. He pressed a noisy kiss on the top of Anthony's head. "Happy birthday."

Anthony shoved him away, laughing, and his sisters came up to get their own hugs and kisses from Max.

"Can you stay? We're playing Aggravation," Jessica said. She was fourteen, but she hadn't outgrown family game nights like most of the teenagers Max knew. He hoped she never would.

"Maybe just a quick round?" Danny said. "It's only an hour and a half to the Pack house."

The kitchen erupted in laughter, leaving Danny with a look of startled confusion.

"We play a little differently than you're probably used to," Max said. "There's no such thing as a quick round of Aggravation in the Torres family."

"They play for money," Kathleen said, shaking her head. "And they're ruthless. Even the kids."

Danny turned to Max. "We're talking about the kids' game, right? With all the colored marbles and the holes in the board you move around?"

Max put his hands on Danny's shoulders and steered him out of the kitchen. "Yes. I'll explain in the car. If you start down this road with them, we'll miss moonrise. Say goodbye to Danny, guys."

Danny returned the chorus of goodbyes as Max steered him out to the car they'd parked at the curb. Their overnight bags were in the trunk, since they'd planned to leave straight from the party.

Alpha Connoll had invited them to run with them and spend the weekend at the Pack compound on the edge of the Sterling Forest State Park. Max was excited to check it out. He wouldn't be able to afford anything big enough to accommodate the whole Pack at once like Alpha Connoll's compound, but he wanted to get a feel for how something like that was set up. It would be nice to have a permanent home base for Pack runs.

"So, playing kids' games for money?" Danny prompted when Max had pulled away from the house.

"It's sounds off the wall, but I swear it's fun. My family puts money on pretty much all the board games we play. I learned to count losing all my good Halloween candy to Pop playing blackjack. We're not allowed to play Monopoly anymore. Ma banned it in the nineties when Phil stabbed one of our cousins with his claws."

Danny shook his head. "I'd love to see it."

"Oh, you will. It's a Torres tradition. We have a board-game night at least once a month with most of the family. Trust me, you'll get the hang of it pretty fast. It usually ends when someone throws the board. Last time we played Aggravation, it was Kathleen. So even though you're not Torres by birth, you can be taught."

"That sounds weirdly aggressive but also fun," Danny said.

Max reached over and squeezed his knee. "That could be my family motto."

Chapter Eleven

MAX was fast. Granted, Danny only ran once a month in his shifted form, so he was out of practice. But even adjusting for that, Max was *fast*. Only Alpha Connoll and Jackson could keep up with him. The three of them were practically a blur in the distance, racing each other to the lake.

He'd googled pictures of binturongs so he'd know what to expect Max's shifted form to look like, but it hadn't prepared him. Those things were small and almost cuddly, with whiskers longer than their faces and long bushy tails that curled around them when they walked. Danny hadn't been too far off with his grizzly comparison. Max was massive. He did have the fluffy tail, though. One Danny wanted to pet some time when he was sure Max wouldn't bite him for trying.

Danny dropped back and trotted alongside Sloane, who didn't like the feel of the soil beneath her paws, so she always minced her steps. Running with Sloane was like watching a wolf play Frogger, jumping between patches of foliage or piles of dead leaves whenever she could.

This run was so different from the ones he'd been on in the past. Before, it had been a chore. Something he did because his body needed to do it, not because his mind enjoyed it. But now that he was more connected with his wolf and his wolf senses, the forest was a fascinating place. The dirt Sloane hated was rich and loamy, and the dry leaves she jumped through made his nose twitch. He could smell his Pack all around him, their scents mixing with pine sap and fresh night air and making him feel invincible with every lungful he drew.

Would it be like this with Max's Pack too? The thrum through the Pack bond filled him up in a way he hadn't known he needed, and he was reluctant to lose that after he'd just found it.

He led Sloane through the trees, following Max's trail. Danny's wolf was half-drunk on the heady scent of its mate. Max smelled the same in shifted form as he did when he was human, but it was amplified. He radiated power and authority. It had been all Danny could do not to bare his neck to him when he'd shifted, but that would have been a grave insult to Alpha Connoll during a full-moon Pack run, so Danny had reeled himself back in.

Sloane nipped at his leg, and Danny turned to look at her. He hadn't realized he'd sped up as he chased after Max's scent, but Sloane was panting and giving him a murderous glare. Danny wasn't out of breath at all. He wondered if that was a benefit of the bond too. He'd never had this kind of stamina before. Did an Alpha Mate get a power boost?

Sloane snapped at him again, and Danny stopped. She shifted, and Danny turned his face away. Nudity was a normal part of Pack life, but he was about crotch level with her in his wolf form, and there were some things a cousin didn't need to see.

He closed his eyes and concentrated, but he couldn't hear anyone. The nearest Pack member had to be at least a quarter mile away.

Danny shifted and turned around. "Did you need something, or are you just being pissy because we're actually running this time?"

Sloane made a face at him. "I wanted to talk to you while we had some privacy."

Standing naked in the middle of a state park wasn't his idea of the best place to talk, but he motioned for her to continue.

"Are you leaving the Pack for real? I heard you and Alpha Connoll talking about it earlier. You're joining Max's Pack permanently?"

Shit. He'd meant to talk to her about it before she found out through the grapevine. He'd told her he intended to switch, but he hadn't put a timeline on it then because he hadn't been sure it was the right move.

"He's planning to do the ritual at the next moon."

Sloane looked away, and Danny caught the salty smell of her tears. "I'm happy for you."

"They're a great Pack," Danny said.

He hesitated, wondering if he should tell Sloane that Max was planning to invite her to join as well. It was really Max's place to do it, but she was upset, and Danny didn't want to cause her any unnecessary angst. Fuck it. He was going to be Pack's Alpha Mate—he could extend an invitation too.

"We'd be honored if you would consider joining the Pack as well," he said. The word *we* hung clumsy and strange on his tongue, but it felt right in his heart. "You'd make a great addition to the Torres Pack."

"You can't invite a stranger to a Pack you haven't even officially joined yet," Sloane said.

"Max and I have already talked about it. He was planning to invite you after I joined. You're family, Sloane. If you want to join my Pack, you can join my Pack."

"I'll think about it," she said after a few beats of silence. "Uncle Daniel is thinking about leaving the Pack too."

He hadn't spoken to his father since the blowup in the lobby. He'd seen his mother once, but she'd been more focused on learning about him than talking about his father. Danny knew his father's loathing for the Pack was bad, but he hadn't realized it was *that* bad.

"Max would never let him join," he said quietly.

Sloane's laugh was bitter and sharp. "Uncle Daniel wouldn't be caught dead in a shifter Pack. You know that. He'd be unaffiliated."

Alpha Connoll would never allow that. His father was an Alpha, which meant the only way he could stay in this territory was as a rank-and-file member of someone else's Pack. An unaffiliated Alpha in New York City would set Supe tongues wagging everywhere, and Danny could think of at least four groups that wouldn't allow it.

"Has he talked to Alpha Connoll about it?"

"No. Aunt Veronica is trying to talk sense into him. It's been different since the gala, Danny. She stands up to him more than I've ever seen. She won't hear a bad word about you. Or me, for that matter."

Danny could have used that when he'd been a kid, but better late than never. Especially if it was helping

Sloane. He knew his parents were here, but only because Alpha Connoll had told him when he and Max had arrived. Apparently they'd chosen to stay in a cabin instead of in the main house like they normally did.

They were here because Alpha Connoll required attendance at the Pack moon runs, but he didn't require anyone to actually run. Most did, but Danny's family often didn't. He and Sloane usually made a somewhat ceremonial attempt, gathering with everyone and running a bit before looping back and spending the rest of the night at the house waiting for everyone to return.

There would be a huge meal around sunrise, and then everyone would find a place to sleep for a few hours. They usually had breakfast for lunch in the late afternoon before everyone started to trickle out to return to the city.

He used to hate full-moon nights because they left him exhausted. But this was different. Exhilarating. If resisting the moon's pull felt like draining a battery, embracing it was like getting a recharge. He had more energy than he knew what to do with. Suddenly it made sense why the wolves who came back from the all-night run were perky and refreshed, even though they hadn't slept.

"I'm going to head back to the house," Sloane said.

He didn't want to maroon her there with nothing to do, but he also wanted to catch up to Max so they could run together.

Sloane laughed at his indecision, which he knew was written all over his face. "It's okay. I brought my textbooks. You should stay out here. I'll see you when we all meet up to eat."

She shifted and trotted off toward the house. Danny shifted as well. He'd never enjoyed the process of going wolf before, and he didn't particularly enjoy it now. But he was faster than ever, probably because he wasn't focused on the pain of it. He wanted to go find Max.

Without Sloane slowing him down, Danny flew through the forest, wind ruffling his thick fur as he rocketed toward Max. It wasn't that his human worries disappeared when he was a wolf, but it was easier to lose them for an hour or two when he gave himself over to it. His instincts were more feral, and his senses were overwhelmed by the smells and sounds of the forest. Getting to Max was at the forefront of his mind, but that didn't mean he'd forgotten about the text he'd gotten from an unknown number on the drive up. It had been signed Sulkie, which was the nickname Danny had given Joss when they'd first started working together and Joss had been a moody preteen. Joss had warned him to stop going to pawn shops, but it hadn't sounded like a threat. It had been more pleading. He was worried about Danny getting too deep into something dangerous.

Danny snorted, which sounded the same in both his wolf and human forms. If Joss thought for a second that Danny would leave him in a situation that he admitted would be too dangerous for an adult, he had another think coming. Actually, he had *Danny* coming. Because the private detective said she was positive she was close to finding an address for him, and once she did, nothing was going to stop Danny from going in after him.

Max's howl shook Danny out of his thoughts. He was close, closer than he'd realized. Danny took off at a sprint, his heart thundering in his chest. It was his turn to run with Max, and he couldn't wait.

Max was alone when Danny caught up with him. The rest of the Pack was nearby, but they were giving Max a wide berth as an unfamiliar Alpha. Danny didn't care—it meant he had Max to himself. He darted forward and nipped at Max's hind leg, drawing a noise that sounded almost like a laugh from him. Max turned and pounced, making easy work of catching Danny and pinning him to the ground.

Danny squirmed his way out, fully aware that the only reason he escaped was because Max let him. Power poured off of Max in this form. Instead of making him cower, it made Danny feel ten feet tall. This glorious, powerful creature was *his* mate, and he was done fighting it.

Everything was so much simpler in shifted form. He was himself, but he didn't feel any shame giving himself over to his baser instincts. He wanted Max, and that was enough. His wolf didn't care about moving too quickly or losing part of himself by bonding to an Alpha—it knew that Max was its mate, and that was enough for Danny to bare his neck and present himself to his Alpha.

His instinctual posture must have been the right choice because Max nipped lightly at his neck and shot up, circling around Danny twice before taking off into the trees. Danny followed, his muscles burning as he strained to keep up. He lost sight of Max twice, but he didn't panic. His scent trail was like a beacon. Danny had no trouble following it.

He stopped short when he realized Max had led them back to the main house. He shifted and walked into the house naked, his human nose still easily able to distinguish Max's scent. Sloane sat hunched over a pile of books and notes at the kitchen counter.

"He's upstairs," she said without looking up. "If you're going to do what I think you're going to do, please take it outside."

He laughed and ran up the stairs, following his nose to a room on the second floor with a closed door. Danny opened it and slipped inside, then closed it behind

himself. The Pack didn't spend a lot of time here, so
the rooms weren't soundproofed like the apartments at
the Pack compound in the city were. Sloane would be
able to hear anything that happened.

Max was pulling blankets off the bed, naked in the
moonlight. He had dirt on his face and his gorgeous
body was sheened with sweat.

"If we do this, there's no going back," he said
softly. He studied Danny's face, a slight frown causing
wrinkles on his forehead.

Instead of responding, Danny crossed the room
and kissed him, pouring everything he could into the
kiss. Max dropped the blanket and wrapped him in a
tight embrace.

"Listen to my heart," Danny said once they broke
for air. He took Max's hand and put it over his chest for
good measure. "I want to bond with you."

Max's eyes flared amber and fluttered shut as he
took in a deep breath. They were still glowing when he
opened them again.

"I won't claim you in another Alpha's house," Max
growled past a mouth full of shifted teeth.

A thrill shot down Danny's spine at the sheer need
in Max's voice. He grinned.

"Better catch me, then," he teased. He grabbed the
blanket and sprinted for the door, slamming it behind
him to give him a few seconds' head start. He tore out
of the house, tempted to go wolf for more speed. The
blanket would be a pain to carry that way, though, and
they definitely needed it for what he had planned.

There was a lake in the woods, and he pointed himself
toward it, running as hard as he could. Max could have
overtaken him by now if he wanted, and Danny loved that
he was playing along and not tackling him where he stood.

The grass was soft and damp near the edge of the water, and Danny laid out the blanket on the bank. It wouldn't be as comfortable as a bed, but it was far enough from the house and the Pack to give them some privacy. He didn't want an audience for his mating bite.

Danny was already sprawled out on the soft fabric when Max pounced on him. He'd regained control of his shift, though his eyes were still rimmed with amber when he straddled Danny and kissed him with a breathless fervor that made Danny's stomach swoop.

"I want this so much," Max murmured. "I want *you* so much."

Danny moved his hips, bringing their cocks into alignment. He hissed out a breath at the touch of Max's velvety skin against his. He'd explored every inch of Max's body already, but this felt new and exciting. His skin hummed with energy, like his entire body was waiting for the bond to complete.

Fuck. He'd been so caught up in the idea of Max chasing him that he hadn't thought to grab lube.

He groaned when Max leaned in to kiss him again. The new position put additional pressure on his cock, and Danny pumped his hips, desperate for more. He could have screamed in frustration when Max pushed himself up, removing what little friction Danny had been able to find.

"Need to come together for the bond," Max said. He sat back on his heels, and Danny edged up on his elbows so he could see him.

The light from the full moon reflected off Max's chest, and Danny watched as the light played over it, deepening the shadows and throwing every muscle into gorgeous relief. Max looked like he'd been carved out of stone, and Danny ached to touch him.

He sat up, relieved when Max made no move to evade him as he reached out for him. Max nuzzled against his neck, his stubble dragging across Danny's skin with just enough bite to make him shiver.

"Gonna put my bite here," Max whispered, pressing a kiss to the juncture of Danny's neck and shoulder. He nipped at it with human teeth, and Danny panted and pressed up into the contact.

"You like that?" Max purred and laved at the spot with his tongue. "Does the thought of my mark on you make you hard?"

God, it did. Danny whimpered, and Max wrapped his arms around him and kissed his jaw. "Don't worry. You won't have to wait long."

Danny's eyes widened at the crack of a cap opening. Max had a bottle of lube. Oh thank God.

Max chuckled. "I told you I'd always take care of you. Did you think I'd consummate our mating bond without making sure I didn't hurt you?"

Of course he wouldn't. Max had done everything he could to look out for Danny since the moment they'd met. His very own Alpha asshole, who turned out not to be much of an asshole at all.

"Alpha," he murmured, knowing it would drive Max crazy.

Max's eyes flared, and he captured Danny's mouth in another insistent kiss. Danny leaned into Max when he felt Max's fingers slide down his crack, lubed and ready. His blood heated as Max's fingers slid over his entrance, and Danny rutted against Max, ready to be filled.

Max eased him down onto the blanket without breaking their kiss. Danny had never felt so desired before. Max's need for him poured through the bond. Danny's emotions—love, amazement, happiness so bright it made his heart hurt—threatened to overwhelm him, but he tuned it all out and focused on the feel of Max's fingers against his skin.

He squeezed his eyes shut when Max pushed into him. There was no gentleness, but Danny didn't want any. There would be plenty of time for foreplay later—the bond needed to be consummated before the fire pulsing through Danny burned him from the inside out. Max was experiencing the same thing. It reverberated through the bond, a feedback loop of raw need, but he'd retained enough control to hold Danny close and whisper how perfect Danny was as he built them toward a frenzied climax.

Just when Danny was afraid he couldn't take any more, Max sank his shifted fangs into his neck. Danny tensed, expecting pain, and cried out in surprise as pleasure so intense it forced the air from his lungs crescendoed to a peak. He couldn't tell where his body ended and Max's began. He came hard, squeezing around Max until he followed suit. The aftershocks made him shake, tears filling his eyes because it felt so good it almost hurt.

"Holy fuck," he whispered when Max finally stilled and buried his face against Danny's neck. "That was.... Fuck."

Max laughed against his neck. "How did I get so lucky to have such an eloquent mate?"

Danny grinned. "You're going to call me mate every time you talk, aren't you?"

Max pressed a kiss against his throat. "Yes, because you *are* my mate. I want everyone to know it."

There wasn't much chance of anyone not knowing exactly what they'd done. Max had marked him, both with the mating bite and by mingling their scents so well that even a human nose could pick out the smell of sex.

Max rolled to the side, bringing Danny with him so they were facing each other on their sides. "You okay?"

"Are you fishing for compliments? Because I think it's pretty obvious I'm awesome."

Max's smile was soft. "I meant about the bond. Does it feel any different being on this side of it?"

It felt amazing. He didn't have any regrets. Danny had spent his adult life ignoring his wolf instincts, but he was embracing them now. His wolf had no doubt that Max was his mate, and for once Danny was going to listen. The bond he and Max shared from day one was undeniable, and Danny was going to trust that his instincts wouldn't lie.

"So different. But in a good way."

Max beamed. He threw back his head and howled, and they both laughed when dozens of wolves answered. Danny was still in the Connoll Pack for now, but he was mated to Alpha Torres. They both had claim to him, but instead of making him anxious, it made him feel loved and wanted. Neither would do anything to abuse their power over him, and this time next month he'd be a full-fledged member of the Torres Pack. He'd never have to answer to another Alpha again, not even Max. It was almost as intoxicating as the bond.

WHAT time do we need to leave for the museum thing tonight?"

They were almost back to the city, and Danny had spent most of the drive thinking about how he could help Joss if he was able to find him today. If Max hadn't reminded him, he'd have forgotten the fundraiser they were supposed to attend with his parents.

"It starts at eight, but it's just cocktails and mingling, so I'd say we could safely arrive around nine and not raise any eyebrows."

"Uncle Al will be there," Max said. "I didn't even ask him to come. It's one of his personal charities. What is it for again?"

Danny had to think. They were halfway through the gauntlet of parties and fundraisers he'd promised his parents they'd attend, and it was difficult to distinguish one from another. It was always the same people, the same type of food, the same boredom.

"I think it's a fundraiser for the summer arts camp they do," he said finally. "Scholarships for kids who can't afford it."

"I can get behind that," Max said. "And you said this one's not formal, right?"

"You can probably get away with that vest I made you change out of when we went to Montauk. It's upscale but not black tie."

"I swear it's like rich people have their own language. I had to have Uncle Al talk me through 'garden-party attire' for the tea your mother is hosting."

There hadn't been enough time to organize anything huge, thank God, so his mother had settled on an intimate gathering of 120 for her Janus Foundation fundraiser. That nightmare wasn't for a few weeks, so it wasn't really on Danny's radar yet.

"I wish you wouldn't worry so much about that stuff," Danny said. "It's not like it's a huge deal."

Max huffed out a laugh. "Spoken like a guy who already knows how to dress and how to act at these things. I spend most of the meals terrified I'm going to cause half the table to faint if I use the wrong knife."

"No one will faint," Danny said, grinning despite his foul mood. "Clutch their heirloom pearls, maybe. But no one would be so gauche as to *faint*."

"See? I don't even own any pearls. I'm hopeless."

Danny dissolved into laughter, his stress over finding Joss eased a bit by Max's playful mood. He wished he could just enjoy this time with Max instead of waiting for the other shoe to drop, but Max was too good to be true. They were ridiculously compatible, more so every day as the bond continued to deepen their connection. No doubt Max had sensed Danny's anxiety, hence the teasing to cheer him up.

"Maybe I can pick some up for you while I'm out today." Danny hadn't told Max he was trying to find Joss. Guilt swept through him at the lie, even though it was a lie by omission. But he couldn't risk Max finding Joss first. He was a cop, and Joss had committed a crime. There was no way Danny would press charges, but if he'd stolen from Danny, he'd probably stolen from other people. They wouldn't be as forgiving.

"Or you could make one yourself later," Max said, turning to wiggle his eyebrows at Danny.

"God, that was terrible," Danny groaned. "Jesus. Thanks for that. Now I'm going to be thinking about cum every time I see a string of pearls."

Max's laugh was rich and deep, and the sheer happiness in it made Danny warm down to his bones.

"That's going to make tonight really interesting, then."

Danny's phone lit up with an incoming text, and he glanced at it, trying to keep his heartbeat steady when he saw it was from the number he was sure was Joss's. He'd texted it last night to tell Joss he'd be back in town today and wanted to meet up at their favorite diner.

Bad idea.

Danny frowned. *I'm going to meet up with you one way or another. Might as well get a free meal out of it.*

"Something wrong?"

Danny pasted on a smile for Max. "I'm meeting a friend for a late lunch, and we can't agree on where to go."

Fine. But leave your new cop boyfriend at home, or we'll both be sorry. I'm serious, pls Danny.

How did Joss know about Max? What the hell had that kid gotten himself into?

His anxiety must have spiked, because Max took a hand off the wheel and cupped the back of his neck. The warmth of his palm seemed to travel down Danny's spine. The tight muscles in his shoulders and back eased, and the tension headache that had been building in his temples faded away to nothing.

The warmth receded as soon as Max let go, but the pain didn't come back.

"What the hell was that?" Danny asked, swiveling in his seat to look at Max. "Did you do some freaky Alpha mojo on me or something?"

"No! Of course not. You smelled like pain, and you looked uncomfortable. I thought it would help."

"What did you *do*, though?"

Max's knuckles went white as he squeezed the steering wheel. "It's a mate thing, I don't know. I've seen my parents do it to each other a million times. I figured it was simply a show of support or something. Why?"

Danny blew out a breath, the adrenaline rush from his anger fading. "You healed my headache. Your hand heated up on my neck, and suddenly my headache was gone and my muscles relaxed."

"Are you serious? What the hell?"

Max's expression was dumbfounded, and Danny believed him. He settled into his seat, suddenly exhausted. The sleepless night had been bound to catch up with him at some point.

"I'm sorry. I—"

"You thought it was some Alpha control thing," Max said, his voice weary. "I get it. I don't.... It wasn't. And I won't do it again unless you ask me to."

Danny knew his reaction had hurt Max. He could smell the bitter stink of it, but he didn't know how to make it better. He wished he could flip a switch and all his Alpha issues would go away, but life didn't work like that.

"I'm trying," Danny said quietly. He let out a sigh of relief when Max reached a hand out and took his. "I know you're not that kind of Alpha. I do."

Max brought Danny's hand up to his mouth and kissed it softly. "I know. It's fine. We both overreacted. It happens. And it doesn't help that the bond is creating a sense of intimacy that our brains haven't caught up with yet. We'll get there."

Max released his hand, and they spent the last twenty minutes of the drive in comfortable silence. It helped recharge Danny's energy a bit, as did the shower he took when he got back to his apartment. The diner he was meeting Joss at was between his place and the foundation, close enough to walk on a nice day.

He was always grumpy the day after a full moon, and his worry for Joss wasn't helping things. The walk would help him clear his head. He needed to be firing on all cylinders when he talked with Joss. The kid was incredibly bright, and if Danny wasn't careful, he'd run circles around him and leave Danny as much in the dark as ever.

He couldn't let that happen. Every kid he worked with was special, and they all deserved a better lot in life than they'd been given. But Joss was different. He was the first Janus Foundation charge that Danny had connected with, and Danny would do anything he could to give Joss a shot at the future he deserved. They were so close. They should be meeting to talk about college applications, not to talk about getting Joss out of whatever mess he'd gotten dragged into.

Danny was shocked to see Joss waiting inside at their usual table. Relief swept through him as he hurried inside. Joss didn't look much the worse for wear. Tired and a little rumpled, but he was clean and well fed. He hadn't been sleeping on the streets the whole time he'd been missing.

"You've gotta call off that lady cop," Joss said when Danny slid into the booth. "She's going to get me killed with her questions."

The private investigator Danny had hired. She wasn't a cop, of course, but Joss wouldn't know that— nor would it make a difference to whoever Joss was tangled up with.

Danny held Joss's gaze and inhaled. He smelled fear, even though there wasn't a visible threat. What he didn't smell was more telling, though. Joss's usual salt-and-ocean-air scent was dull. Stale.

"Who has your skin, Joss?" he asked quietly.

Tears welled in Joss's eyes. "You have to leave it alone, Danny. I'm begging you. You can't get involved. They'll kill you."

It all made sense now. Joss was a selkie. If someone had managed to kidnap his seal hide, he'd be bound to them until he could get it back.

"Are they hurting you?"

Joss shook his head. "They haven't done anything to it yet, but they will if that lady keeps asking questions."

Fuck. Danny took out his phone. "I'll tell her to stop," he said, sending her a text explaining why.

He didn't need her anymore anyway. He'd hired her to find Joss, and here he was.

"What are they making you do? How can we get your skin back?"

Joss closed his eyes and hunched in on himself. "We can't. They've got witches. A lot of them. And they've got our skins warded."

Our? Shit. This was bigger than just Joss, then. "How many?"

"Selkies? Eight? Ten? Something like that. They've got at least that many witches too. They help us get past security systems and cameras and shit. At first it was okay because we were careful and no one got hurt," Joss said, his voice breaking.

"But that changed last week when they started killing people," Danny finished for him. Fuck. This was worse than he thought. He'd assumed Joss owed someone money. He hadn't tied it to the crime ring Max was investigating.

Max.

Danny had to let him know they were Supes. He picked up his phone again, but Joss closed a hand over his wrist, stopping him.

"I'm sorry, Danny," he said, tears spilling over, terrified gaze pinned over Danny's shoulder. "They must have followed me. I swear I didn't know. I'm so sorry."

Danny registered the sound of a vehicle jumping the curb a split second before the glass front of the diner shattered. He could barely hear the customers screaming over the roar of the engine as the van tore through the restaurant.

His nose twitched, and he almost laughed. The world was falling down around his ears, and he was overcome with the urge to sneeze. There was a thick ozone smell in the air, overpowering the oil gushing from the car's torn undercarriage and the drywall and other debris clogging his senses. He'd never smelled it before, but he recognized it instinctively.

Magic.

The realization that the witches Joss was so scared of were here had him breaking free of his paralysis. He hurled himself over the Formica table, crashing into Joss and dragging him off the bench seat. He spread himself over Joss, shielding him from the van that slammed into them and pinned them to the wall.

For a second, time seemed to slow down. The engine died, and the diner seemed eerily quiet without the angry hum of gears. The smell of ozone thickened, filling his lungs to the point he couldn't draw a breath. And then it receded just as suddenly, and sound rushed back.

Danny's body erupted in agony. He had to pour all his concentration into holding his human form and not letting himself shift to wolf, and he was dizzy with the effort. Joss was still beneath him, his breathing heavy but unimpeded. Danny rested his head against Joss's shoulder, comforted by each rise and fall of his chest. His own breaths were harsh and painful. It was almost impossible to separate out individual injuries from the white-hot pain that seared through him, but he was reasonably certain he was still in one piece.

"Danny? Holy fuck. Danny? Are you alive?"

Danny wheezed out a confirmation that he wasn't dead, but he couldn't manage much more than that. People had started moving around the diner, doing what they could to help the injured. There were sirens in the distance, and he sent up a fervent prayer they were for them.

He had to get out of here. The scrapes on his face and arms were already healing and he couldn't risk paramedics asking questions. Danny tried to straighten, gasping when the movement sent a new shower of lava through his broken body.

Joss had managed to flip himself around so he could help support Danny's weight.

"What are you doing? Stop. Stop moving, Danny. Fuck, you could have broken your back."

"Gotta go," he gritted out. "Healing."

"Yes, you need help healing. Just stay still."

His broken bones wouldn't heal until they were set correctly, but he couldn't let himself be taken to a hospital. It was something ingrained in wolflings from the moment of their Turn, if not earlier. He repeated it in his head like a mantra to keep himself from passing out. *Secrecy is everything. Don't let humans know what you are.*

The sirens were unbearably loud now. Danny tried one more time to push himself up, but he ended up dry heaving when the movement jarred his dislocated shoulder. He looked into Joss's wide, terrified eyes, and then the world went black.

Chapter Twelve

"I'M not saying the Yankees suck, but—"

Pain lanced through Max, sucking the breath out of him. He doubled over and clutched his ribs. His entire chest was on fire, and there wasn't a single part of him that didn't hurt.

Oscar squatted in front of him, his hands on Max's shoulders.

"Do I need to call a rig? You're scaring me, buddy."

He forced himself to stand up straight. "Call Danny."

Oscar stood with him, still holding on. Max probably would have toppled over without the support. He leaned into Oscar, letting his partner bear his weight.

"I'm calling this in," Oscar said, one arm looped around Max.

"Call Danny," he repeated, his voice stronger this time. The pain had faded, but he was still wobbly and weak.

"Unless Danny has an MD after his name, he's not the one you need to see right now. What hurts, Max? You were holding your chest. Is it your heart?"

It was, but not the way Oscar meant. Something had happened to Danny. Something horrible. Mate bonds could transmit strong emotions when one of the bonded pair was in trouble, and Alpha Mate bonds were even more intense. This wasn't Max's pain. It was *Danny's*.

"I'm okay. I just need to check in with Danny."

Oscar gave him a dirty look but dialed Danny's number anyway. It went straight to voicemail. Now he knew something was wrong. Danny never turned his phone off. He needed to be available at all times for the foundation. He didn't even turn it off when he was in court.

"I'll leave him a message when we get you to the hospital and we know what's going on." Oscar started pulling Max toward the car. They'd been heading out to do surveillance on a warehouse that was next on the list to be robbed, according to a call that had come in on the tip line.

Fuck. Danny had been cagey about who he was meeting for lunch, and Max had let it go because he didn't want to come across as a possessive boyfriend. Whatever was going on had to be tied to whoever he was meeting.

Max let Oscar shepherd him into the car without protest, but he had no intention of going to the hospital to get checked out. There wasn't anything wrong with him.

His fingers shook as he dialed Sloane's number, and he could have cried in relief when she picked up.

"Do you know where Danny is?"

Sloane hesitated. "He had errands today or something."

Max forced himself to take a breath so he didn't scream at her. "Something's wrong, Sloane. He's in trouble. I need to know where he is."

"I don't know, Max."

"I'm not fucking around," he snapped. He looked at Oscar, who was driving but clearly listening in on the conversation. He probably thought Max had had a psychotic break or something. "You know how I have that, uh, psychic cousin? Well, I got the same kind of, um, vision that she does. It was like I could feel what was happening to Danny, and it wasn't good."

Sloane caught on, thank God. "Shit. He's been trying to find one of his kids. He thinks he's the one who stole the foundation stuff."

Papers shuffled in the background. "I'm going to text you the contact information for the private investigator he was using. She might know where he was going. Oh my God, Max. What do you think happened to him? What do you mean you felt his pain?"

She was close to tears, and as angry as he was that she'd been helping Danny go behind his back to interfere with his investigation, he couldn't leave her in the dark.

"You know what it means. We share a tight bond, remember?" Her intake of breath reassured him she'd gotten his point. "I'll find him. Keep trying to call him, okay? Let me know if you get him."

He called the number she sent him, but that was an office phone that went straight to voicemail. He left a clipped, angry message and his callback information and hung up, tossing the phone on the dashboard in disgust. His mate needed him and he was absolutely useless. Damnit.

"Since when do you have a psychic cousin?" Oscar asked, his tone heated.

"Probably since she was born, I don't know how that shit works," Max snapped. His control was threadbare right now, and it wouldn't take much to push him over the edge. He closed his eyes, hoping they weren't flashing.

His phone rang before Oscar could ask another question, and he grabbed it with preternatural speed, not even trying to tone it down for the human in the car. At this rate he was going to have to confess everything to Oscar or risk his partner investigating on his own.

His heart sank when he his brother's name lit up the screen. "Phil? It's not a—"

"You've got to get over here. EMTs just brought Danny in, and he's in bad shape. I'm working on him, and he'll be okay, but it's going to be hard to cover this up."

Phil hung up, and Max's heart fell to his feet.

"It's Danny. Phil's working on him in his ER." He took a shaky breath. "Full siren."

Max's parents were already there when he and Oscar burst through the ER entrance. He'd tried to get Oscar to drop him off, but he'd refused. They'd double parked in a fire lane, lights still running, on their dash to the ER.

He'd have to convince Oscar to go park it in the hospital garage to buy them some time to get their story straight before Oscar saw Danny. Max hated that he had to think about that right now when all he wanted to do was see that his mate was safe, but he had a duty not just to Danny but to his Pack and the greater supernatural community to make sure their secret didn't get out.

Oscar was on his heels as he skidded up to the nurse's station, but he stopped when Max's mom called out to him. She had her arm around a lanky teenager Max didn't recognize, but he didn't have time to stop. He kept going past them, making a beeline for the front desk.

"You have my husband here," he said, deciding Danny would forgive the lie because of the circumstances. "Daniel Cresswell."

The nurse didn't bat an eye. "Dr. Torres told us to expect you. Kim will take you back right away."

Thankfully, Oscar didn't try to follow. Max wasn't sure what he was going to find when he got to Danny.

He could be shifted, and at the very least he'd be healing at an inexplicable rate.

The nurse was a fast walker, which he appreciated. Max didn't need her to find Danny, but he let her lead because running through the ER would bring more unwanted attention. Hospitals were always rough, with the stringent bite of antiseptic and the scent of pain and sickness, but smelling Danny's blood—and not just a little of it—made Max's control falter. He shoved his hands in his pockets to conceal the claws that were sprouting and kept his head down in case his eyes were glowing.

Breathing through his mouth helped mute the overwhelming scents, and Max zeroed in on Danny's heartbeat to help keep him grounded. It was faster than normal but steady.

Phil was bandaging Danny's left leg when Max walked into the room. The nurse closed the door behind him, and Max lunged for Danny. Phil stopped him with a hand to his chest.

"I haven't been able to set his broken bones because there's no curtain over the window," Phil said, nodding over Max's shoulder. "I want to do it while he's still out because it will be horrifically painful, and I can't give him anything for it."

Fuck. Max needed to hold Danny so badly that it was physically painful to be separated from him, but he could handle that. He was more worried about Danny's pain.

"What do you need me to do?"

"Stand in front of the door. Lean your back against the window. Don't let anyone in."

Max took his position, leaning hard against the door. He put his hand on the doorknob for good measure.

"Brace yourself. He's probably going to wake up, and it's not going to be pretty. I need to be focused on Danny, so you have to control yourself, okay? You can't hulk out in here."

"Danny calls it going asshole Alpha," Max murmured.

"Well, whatever you call it, you can't do it. He'll respond to your emotions, so if you lose it, he'll probably shift. That's a problem we don't need. Got it?"

This was going to be torture for him, but it was going to be worse for Danny. Max could be strong for him. And he trusted his brother. If Phil said this was necessary, then it was.

Max tightened his stance, his muscles tensing as he waited for Phil to begin. He closed his eyes for good measure. Hearing and smelling Danny in pain was bad enough.

"I will haunt you forever if you freak out and kill me for hurting your mate," Phil said under his breath. "Okay. One, two, three."

Danny drew in a harsh breath and started screaming. Max's fangs dropped, and he could barely contain a growl. He held his breath until his lungs burned, which was a mistake. As soon as he took a breath and the scent of Danny's pain filled his nostrils he lost control of the shift. Fire rippled over his skin as he sprouted fur. He kept his back pressed against the door, using the connection with it to rein himself in. He wanted to rip Phil away from his mate, but rationally he knew Phil wasn't hurting Danny on purpose. He was setting bones so Danny could heal properly.

"Fuck," Danny muttered, his voice hoarse.

Max's eyes shot open, and his shift receded as quickly as it had come on. He forced himself to wait until Phil nodded before he hurled himself across the small space. Danny was propped up in the bed with one leg immobilized and his right arm in a sling.

"Jesus Christ," Max whispered. He wanted to touch Danny but he couldn't find a part of him that didn't look battered. His clothes were ripped, and he was covered in a grimy layer of dust and blood.

Danny held his left hand out, and Max grabbed it. The skin-on-skin contact helped the last of his shift recede and cleared the haze in his head.

"Did they bring anyone with me? Tall, light brown hair? I covered him from the worst of it, but he could be hurt. We need to find him."

Panic tinged Danny's words, and Max's gut tightened. Was this the friend Danny had been meeting?

Phil looked at the chart. "A guy rode in with you in the bus. EMTs checked him for injuries, and he was okay. Covered in blood, but they assumed it was yours. Is he a shifter?"

"Selkie," Danny said. He let go of Max's hand and struggled to get up. "Where is he now? Is he here? He's got to be terrified."

Phil put a gentle hand to Danny's chest and Danny deflated like an old balloon, sinking back against the bed with a groan.

"You're not going anywhere. The bones I set are still healing." Phil dropped the chart in the sink and turned on the water.

"I left the chart on the edge of the sink and it fell in while I was washing my hands after checking on you," he said, giving Danny a significant look. "We'll do our best to recreate it, but I won't be able to remember exactly what the EMTs said when they brought you in. What I remember is going to include a lot of things like "tenderness" and "possible broken bones." If anyone else comes in to examine you, we're going to go with bruised ribs and a bad knee sprain. You had a CT scan while you were out, and it confirmed a severe concussion, so tell them about headache and nausea. Sensitivity to sounds and lights won't be hard to fake."

"I have to find Joss," Danny said. He winced when he tried to lift his injured leg, and this time Max was the one to restrain him. He wasn't going to let Danny hurt himself.

"Joss Collins?" he asked sharply.

Danny tensed, and Max had to clench his teeth to keep in a flurry of profanity.

"Are you kidding me, Danny? That kid was identified on a traffic cam outside one of the warehouse robberies. How do you know Collins? Why were you meeting with him?"

"He's one of mine," Danny said, his eyes bright with unshed tears. "He's not in it willingly. I've been trying to find him for weeks. He's a good kid, Max. He's mixed up with witches, and they're making him steal things."

Max swallowed hard and took a step away from the bed. He wanted to wring Danny's neck for putting himself in danger and interfering with a police investigation, but he also wanted to crush him to his chest and never let him go. He'd never been so scared before in his life. Not even when Ray almost drowned on that family vacation to the Poconos and Max had to give him CPR.

"They have his skin," Danny croaked. "They're holding it hostage. He *had* to do what they said, Max. And I don't think he's the only one they're forcing."

Of course. That's why none of the stolen items had shown up on the local black market and why none of his informants had any idea who was behind the thefts. The witches were blackmailing their foot soldiers. That's why no one had gotten light-fingered with a haul or bragged to their buddies about the heists.

They couldn't, or the witches would kill them.

Jesus.

"He's sitting with Ma," Max said.

He leaned in and cradled Danny's face with his free hand, hoping he could ease the pain like he had in the car earlier today. Danny relaxed into the pillows, some of the tightness in his face easing.

"He's just a kid," Danny repeated. The words were pleading this time.

Max squeezed his fingers and pressed a kiss to his temple. "I know. I'm calling Jackson in on this. The Enforcers are going to want a piece of that coven, assuming the Fae Guard doesn't get there first. I'm going to have to talk to Joss, Danny. Can you get him to talk to me, do you think? If I bring him back here?"

Danny shook his head slightly. "He wouldn't tell me anything, Max. I tried. That's what we were doing when the witches attacked. They'd had him followed. He said getting involved would kill us both. I guess he wasn't kidding."

Max squeezed his fingers again. "I won't let anything happen to either of you. But I need a way in. I need to know how they operate and where they're keeping his skin."

Phil cleared his throat, and Max started. He'd forgotten his brother was there. His senses were so trained on Danny, he'd tuned everything else out.

"I'll go get him. I'll tell him Danny wants to see him. If he sees you come for him, he might run, Max."

Phil was right. And it also meant he wouldn't have to let go of Danny, which he definitely wasn't ready to do yet.

"Thanks, Phil."

He leaned his forehead against Danny's when the door shut behind Phil. "I don't know where I can touch you."

"Anywhere," Danny croaked. He shot Max a crooked smile.

"Pervert," Max said affectionately. "I don't want to hurt you. I can't tell where you're hurt."

Danny huffed out a small laugh. "Everywhere. But it's getting better. And touching you helps a lot," he said, wiggling his fingers against Max's palm.

"We're going to talk about you going behind my back with this later," Max warned. "It's—you could have been killed, Danny. You can't go nosing around my cases. You're not a Hardy Boy."

"I've always seen myself more as a Nancy Drew," Danny murmured.

"I'm not joking, Danny. You're messing around with something that's incredibly dangerous."

"He's one of my kids," Danny said, his voice hardening. "What was I supposed to do, Max? Write him off because he's struggling? You know that's not how it works."

"You should have trusted me enough to tell me what you were doing."

"So you could arrest him? Fuck, Max. I love you, but you don't exactly have his best interests at heart. You'd look at him and see a criminal."

Max's angry retort died on his lips. "You love me?"

Danny's eyes widened, but he didn't contradict him.

The door opened before Max could respond. A teenaged blur was on a crash course with the bed, and Max let go of Danny so he could grab Joss around the waist and change his trajectory so he didn't collide with the bed and rattle Danny.

The kid was all elbows as he lashed out, struggling in Max's hold. Danny was shouting the kids name and telling Max not to hurt him.

"I'm not trying to hurt him, I'm trying to stop him from hurting *you*."

"Joss wouldn't hurt me, Max."

The kid stopped fighting, and Max cautiously released him. "Not on purpose, but if I hadn't grabbed him he'd have jumped on the bed. Do you want Phil to have to set your bones again?"

Danny let out a sound that was close to a whimper. "Definitely not."

"Are you okay?" Joss asked, his voice thick. "There was so much blood, and you passed out. I didn't even know Weres *could* pass out."

Danny's smile was weak but genuine. "Learn something new every day, huh, kid?"

"Fuck, Danny. I told you they weren't kidding. I told you."

Joss's voice broke, and he knelt by Danny's bed, head down. Danny couldn't reach him, so Max stepped up and put a hand on the kid's back, rubbing small circles while he sobbed. Danny met Max's eyes, and Max had no problem reading the pleading in them. Danny was still worried Max was going to arrest Joss. Like he'd be worried about that when Danny had been half dead in that bed twenty minutes ago.

Guilt and misery were coming off the kid in waves so strong they choked out the air in the room. Max trusted Danny's judgment on Joss, but even if he didn't, it was clear that the kid had been just as surprised by the attack as Danny had been. If the witches had Joss's skin, then it was a case of coercion. Joss couldn't be blamed for what he'd done. He was just a scared kid.

Of course, Max would have a hell of a time convincing the DA that Joss shouldn't be held responsible for his actions. He'd have to ask Uncle Al to make some calls and quietly get the evidence against Joss dismissed. The kid didn't belong in prison.

"Joss, c'mon," Danny murmured. "Sh. We're okay."

"What about all the other people in the diner?" Joss asked, sniffling. "What about the people they've already killed? I don't know what to do, Danny. I can't leave, but I don't want to do this."

Max squeezed Joss's shoulder. "You don't have to. You know the Werewolf Tribunal? They're sending Enforcers to help me bust the witches. All you need to do is tell me whatever you can remember about them."

Joss's eyes were red and puffy when he looked up. "They'll burn my skin."

"Not if we find it first. The Enforcers are very good at what they do, Joss. Do you have any idea where they're keeping it?"

"I know exactly where they're keeping it," he said with a snarl. "It's warded a million times over. No one gets in there without the coven's permission."

Danny scooted up on the pillows with a groan. "Joss, this isn't helping. You need to answer Max."

"Actually, I think it'll be better if we do this formally," Max said. "Do you think you can give a statement, Joss? And keep magic out of it? Something we can use as a reason to get a search warrant."

"They'll fry you and your warrant," Joss said.

"Not if the Enforcers get in there first and disable the wards," Max said. He'd never worked with them before, but Jackson assured him there wasn't much they weren't capable of.

Joss sat back on his heels. "It's not my fault if your boyfriend gets killed," he warned Danny.

Max held his tongue. The kid was scared out of his mind, and if being a little shit made him feel like he had more control over the situation, then so be it. It was something Max saw often on the streets. Joss would cooperate in the end, but he was going to put up enough of a fight that he had plausible deniability when someone accused him of being a rat.

"Do I need to call a lawyer for him?"

"I'm not looking at him as a suspect anymore," Max said. "We'll cut a deal. I'm sure the DA will agree that it's more important to go after the big fish."

"I want his record sealed," Danny said. "Something like this will follow him for the rest of his life if we're not careful."

"I'll let the DA know. That's not my call."

"Max—"

"It's okay, Danny," Joss said quietly. "Whatever happens, happens. As long as the Enforcers stop the coven, at least we'll all be safe."

"I'm going to take him in later so we can formally question him. He's a ward of the state, so his social worker will need to be there before we can interview him. Right now I'm taking him to meet Jackson so we can talk. Oscar doesn't know who he is, so I'll ask him to stay here in the waiting room while I run home a kid who was in the accident with you. Sound like a plan?"

"If the witches come for me, Oscar won't be able to stop them," Danny said. "Why don't you have him go back to the precinct?"

"I don't want him digging around without me. As for the coven, Phil's here, and so is Ray. They've probably already called reinforcements. They'll take care of you."

He could tell from the tilt of Danny's mouth that he didn't like that, but Max didn't care. His mate had almost been killed today. He was allowed to be a little overprotective. And it wasn't unwarranted. They'd gone after Danny in a public place once today already.

"I'll have Phil text me with updates about when you can go home," Max said. He leaned in and kissed Danny softly. "I don't want you to be alone until this is over. You can stay with me, and if I'm not home, you can stay with someone else."

Danny pursed his lips but nodded.

"Okay. Joss, we're going to Alpha Connoll's compound. Will you be comfortable there? We could meet somewhere else, but if we do it there we won't have to worry about eavesdroppers."

Joss shrugged. "Selkies are nomadic. It doesn't matter whose territory we're in. Not to us, at least."

Chapter Thirteen

"I DON'T need a blanket," Danny protested. He sighed when the tiny woman armed with itchy wool glared at him. "Thank you, Auntie."

She spread the handmade blanket over him, taking care to tuck him in. Danny didn't even know her name, but he'd learned that all older women in the Torres Pack were addressed as auntie. Her face had lost a bit of its scowl when he'd used the honorific, and Danny was left relieved he'd escaped death for a second time in as many days.

Phil had kept him in the hospital overnight, but he'd released him into Sloane's care this morning. She'd brought him to Max's parents' house, since she couldn't miss her residency orientation.

That had been hours ago, and there was still no word from Max. He'd talked to him late last night, and

Max said he was waiting for Jackson to get permission from the Werewolf Tribunal to move in on the coven. The raid was happening today, but Danny was in the dark about the details.

He hated that. He felt so helpless.

His mother had come to see him in the hospital, which had been a shock. She'd cried over him, which had been an even bigger surprise. Danny had never felt so loved. She hadn't argued when he told her he planned to go to Max's parents' house to recover. There was no way his father would allow him into the town house in Manhattan, and he couldn't ask Sloane or his mother to stay with him at his apartment. Not with the coven still on the loose. Max had made sure his Second was there to accompany Danny home. Bert had slept in the room next to Danny's last night.

Joss had slept on the floor right next to the bed. The poor kid was traumatized, and Danny didn't know how to help him. He'd have to get him a new therapist. Maybe Harris or Tate, since they were Connoll Pack members and Joss wouldn't have to edit himself like he would with a human.

"There are like, a ton of people here," Joss said as he wandered in with a plate full of food. He sat near Danny's feet, his weight pulling the blanket even tighter around Danny.

"It's a big Pack. And a big family too."

Danny's head was pounding, but he'd refused when Ray had tried to carry him upstairs to one of the bedrooms. He didn't want to be packed away upstairs. He wanted to be down here where they couldn't hide updates about the raid from him.

"Phil said you needed quiet. Are you sure you don't want to go take a nap? You're not supposed to be straining your brain after you scrambled it."

He'd been given strict instructions not to do anything strenuous for at least twenty-four hours. Officially it was more like seventy-two, but Phil had given him alternate instructions when the nurse was out of earshot.

His bones had healed, but a severe concussion took more time, apparently. Danny felt like fresh hell, but at least he'd been able to leave. Phil was handling the fallout of his miraculous recovery by telling everyone that Danny was a lucky bastard who'd come in covered in other people's blood. Danny wasn't sure how far he was going to get with that, but thanks to the fabricated reports, there was no medical reason to keep him aside from the concussion, and that could be monitored at home as long as he had someone with him.

He had about fifteen someones, which was fourteen more than he'd like. It was sweet the way the Pack kept dropping food by for him, but he could do without the revolving door of concerned well-wishers.

Mrs. Torres insisted that Joss stay with them while his social worker figured out where to place him. The group home he'd been living in wouldn't take him back, and there weren't many foster families who'd take on a seventeen-year-old runaway with a troubled past.

"I don't need a nap. I just need people to whisper," Danny said.

Joss shot him a look of concern. "They are whispering," he said. "This is why you should go upstairs. Ray said the bedrooms are soundproofed."

"I want to stay down here," Danny said firmly.

"I'll come let you know if they hear from Max," Joss said, ignoring him. "I bet he'll text you first anyway. If he does, I'll come read it to you right away."

Joss patted his pocket. Phil had confiscated Danny's phone, which had also survived the crash. He wasn't allowed to read or use any type of screen for the next two days. That meant he couldn't even distract himself with a game of Candy Crush. All he could do was sit and wait to hear how the raid on the coven's warehouse went when Max finally called.

The Enforcers usually worked alone, but they'd let Max and Jackson come along. Danny wished they hadn't. He didn't want to think about all the ways the raid could go wrong.

"He seems pretty great," Joss said. "Max, I mean. He knows his stuff. And you should have heard him on the phone insisting all the charges against me be dropped by the DA. It was wild."

That had gone well at least. Danny was going to have to work overtime to help Joss's social worker find a placement for him, but that had to wait until his jailers gave him back his phone and laptop.

"And Oscar is funny. Dude's got jokes."

Now that he was actually focused on him, Danny realized Joss was babbling because he was nervous. He'd told them where the coven kept the selkie skins they'd stolen, and he had to trust that Max would honor his promise to rescue them. It wasn't only his—Joss said there were at least a dozen pelts in the warded vault.

"What's Oscar doing now?"

"Ah," Joss said, looking away. "He's probably at the station or something."

Danny's senses were still out of whack thanks to his concussion, but it didn't take super hearing for the lie to be obvious.

"Or something, huh?"

Joss wrinkled his nose. "Max told him. He kind of had to, I guess? Oscar said he had fangs and flashing eyes on the drive over to the hospital."

Shit. Poor Max. Like he needed more stress right now. "How did Oscar take it?"

"Better than most humans would," Joss said with a shrug. "He didn't run screaming when Max flashed his eyes at him on purpose. That would make 90 percent of people wet their pants."

It sure would. Especially since Max was an Alpha. "So where is he really?"

"Sitting in a car a few blocks from the warehouse monitoring the police radio so he can give them a heads-up if anyone calls the cops on them."

That was smart. Danny relaxed his death grip on the blanket. Having Oscar watching their back was a good thing.

"They'll be okay," Joss said, pasting on a brave smile. "Have you met that Jackson guy? He's built like a tree. He used to be an Enforcer. If the rest of them are built like him, those witches don't stand a chance."

Danny smiled because it seemed like Joss needed him to. "I've met him. And his husband, who's a great guy."

Joss rolled his eyes. "He's like twice my age. I wasn't perving on him."

Danny had seen Jackson. There was no way Joss hadn't perved just a little. Hell, Danny had perved a lot, both on Jackson and his husband Harris. They were a gorgeous couple. He'd been jealous of them when they joined the Pack. Not that he'd cared that Alpha Connoll had brought in an outsider for the Second position, but because Jackson and Harris seemed so effortlessly in love. It was something he'd been sure he'd never experience, yet here he was.

Joss sat in silence with him for a few minutes, quiet but still managing to be the loudest thing in the room with his fidgeting and his heavy sighs. Danny took a minute and centered himself, like he always did before a therapy session. Joss clearly needed to talk, and Danny wouldn't mind taking some distance from his own brain right now.

"How about we talk about what happened with the coven?"

Joss gave him a sidelong glance. "How about no?"

Danny held up his hands. "Hey, it's up to you. Just think about it, okay? You've been through something traumatic, and you might be struggling with how to process it. I'm here anytime, or if you'd rather see someone else, I can get you in touch with some great psychologists who specialize in Supe patients."

"I'm not the one who almost died! They made me rob some apartments and a few warehouses. No one hurt me."

Danny waited, letting the silence stretch on. Joss broke about forty seconds in.

"They didn't like, mistreat us. We had a place to stay, and they made sure we had food. We could come and go. I wasn't—I'm not the victim here, Danny. I'm the criminal."

Danny made a soft sound. "Would you have stolen things for the coven if they hadn't taken your skin?"

Joss swallowed hard. "No."

"You said you could come and go, but did they threaten you with anything if you didn't come back?"

"If we missed check-in or we weren't there for a job, they said they'd destroy our skins. There was this guy, he was older, like, older than you. He chickened out and didn't go into the warehouse with the others. When we got back they brought out his skin and held a branding iron to it. I've never seen someone in so much pain." Joss blinked away tears. "After that we listened, and no one fucked around. Not the selkies, at least. There were other Supes. I don't know how they controlled them. I'm *glad* I don't know."

Danny wanted to wrap him up in a hug, but he had rules about contact when he had his therapy hat on. He couldn't blur the line—he had to be impassive or he couldn't help them. Some of the things his kids told him in session were horrifying. They had to trust that when they ended the session, he'd be fun-loving, happy Danny for them. Breaking down in the middle of a session and asking for a hug wasn't an option.

"Do you think you'll feel it?" he asked instead. "When they free your skin? Are you connected to it?"

"It's not like I can tell whenever someone touches it. They've had it for weeks, and I've never felt anything. I'd definitely be able to tell if anything bad happened to it. The guy they punished—"

"Tortured," Danny cut in, keeping his voice mild. "Words have power, Joss. They weren't punishing him for misbehaving, they were torturing him. There's a difference. Nothing that happened to any of you while you were at the mercy of the coven was your fault. You didn't do anything wrong. The things they made you do—you were surviving, Joss. You were doing exactly what anyone would have done in your place. You were staying alive."

Joss's inhale was shaky, but he continued his story with a firm voice. "That guy, he got sick. After they'd taken his skin away again and put it with the others, he was still in a lot of pain. And then he had a fever and chills. They took him away on the third day, and he didn't come back. I think they might have killed him."

Danny hated that Joss had to live with that memory. He'd seen enough grief and had enough heartbreak in his short life—it ate Danny up inside to know Joss would be haunted by this too.

"The Enforcers are going to make sure the coven is brought to justice," Danny said with more certainty than he felt.

"And I'll still be a homeless fuckup with a criminal record," Joss muttered.

They both jumped a little when Max's mother walked into the room with a tray of cookies and two big glasses of milk.

"I thought you boys might like a snack," she said, putting the tray on the table. She ran a hand across Danny's forehead like she was checking for a fever, then ruffled his hair and sat next to Joss.

"I know you two have a lot on your minds right now, but I might be able to lessen the burden a bit. Danny knows this, Joss, but you probably don't. My brother is the mayor." She folded her hands in her lap and leaned forward. "He has an ego the size of city hall. I've always hated politics, but Al is a pretty good egg, if you can forgive his abundance of self-esteem. He made a few calls for us, and since Sam and I both had extensive background checks during Al's campaign, he was able to move the paperwork along for us to become a certified foster family. We'll still have to do a home visit and an interview, but the state is allowing us to provide an emergency home for you while all that happens, Joss. If you'd like to stay here, that is. We hope you'll say yes, but I don't want to pressure you. Sam and I are suffering from an empty nest, and I'd love to have someone to feed and fawn over in the house again."

Joss's face crumpled, and this time Danny did move forward and hug him.

"Hey, no. This is a good thing. Do you want to stay here? I'm a little biased, but I can tell you the Torres family is awesome."

"No, I know," Joss said thickly. He pulled away and dashed his tears with his arm. "Thank you, Mrs. Torres. No foster parent has ever said they wanted me before."

There wasn't a dry eye in the living room as Max's mom came over and wrapped her arms around both of them.

"Call me Deenie, sweetheart," she said. "Sam and I would be honored if you'd trust us enough to let us take care of you."

"I appreciate the place to stay, but I don't really need anyone to take care of me. I'm not a kid."

Deenie shushed him. "You haven't had enough time to be a kid, but that doesn't mean you aren't one. This one is still a kid to me too," she said, taking Danny by the chin and squeezing gently. "He needs someone to take care of him, but Max beat me to it. Not that I'm going to pass up any opportunity I get."

She patted his leg. "Eat your snack. The kids are coming for dinner. I'm sure Max will shoo out the rest of the Pack."

The chocolate chip cookie Joss handed him was still hot. Danny took a bite and was surprised to find he was ravenous. He'd been too worried about Max to eat breakfast.

Deenie raised an eyebrow, and he could swear her eyes were twinkling. "I'll bring some sandwiches to tide you over."

Joss cast a worried glance at Danny once she'd left. "Are you okay with me staying here?"

"Why wouldn't I be? They're great, Joss."

"Because this is your boyfriend's family. I don't want to mess this up for you. You know foster families and I don't mix. What if they end up hating you because you brought me into their lives?"

Danny sat up and grabbed for Joss. Stars spun in front of his eyes, but he got a good grip on him and hauled Joss in close.

"Listen. You deserve wonderful things. The problems you've had with other foster families are on them, not you. I've read your case file, Joss. Every problem you've had can be traced back to rotten foster parents or issues you couldn't help. But Deenie and Sam know what you are. You don't have to hide around them. And they're pretty awesome people. You could be happy here if you let yourself."

Joss shrugged and kept his gaze on his feet. He was wearing a pair of Sam's socks, which were covered with kittens and tacos. Joss hadn't had anything with him when they brought him home, so Deenie had rounded up some clothes for him to borrow after herding him upstairs to shower off all the blood and dust from the diner. The socks were so *Sam*, as much so as he and Deenie offering to take in a complete stranger because he needed help. It was such a Torres family kind of thing to do.

Deenie had moved in on him like a mother bear, and Danny didn't think Joss was ever going to be able to extract himself. The thought made him smile.

"I know you think you're old enough to be on your own. Maybe you're right. But give them a chance, okay?"

Deenie called Joss into the kitchen, and Danny kept an ear on them. That was normally rude, but Joss was one of his charges, and he was fragile right now—Danny wasn't taking any chances. It was clear Deenie was fluent in teenage boy, and Danny let himself lose the thread of the conversation and sink back into the pillows once he was sure things were on the right track.

After a while, Joss returned with a plate of sandwiches and two glasses of tea. Deenie seemed committed to keeping them hydrated and fed.

"Alpha Connoll called. I'm going to stay here with Deenie and Sam for now, but he said he'd start the process of getting certified to adopt me if I want," Joss said. He looked a little shell-shocked. "He has a couple selkies in his Pack, and he said his youngest son is only a few years older than me, so he thought I might be comfortable with them."

Danny wasn't surprised. This had his mother's fingerprints all over it. His throat went tight, and he swallowed hard. He didn't want Joss to think he was upset—he wasn't. This was amazing news.

"Alpha Connoll is a great guy," he said. "And I've met his youngest, Ryan. I think you'd like him."

The ghost of a smile curved Joss's lips. "I've always wanted a brother."

"You'll have more than you know what to do with if you take him up on his offer. Alpha Connoll has a couple kids, and they live in a building full of Pack."

Danny caught Max's scent a few seconds before the front door opened. He dropped his sandwich on the scratchy afghan and bolted off the couch. His stomach rolled at the spike of pain in his head, but he ignored it as he raced to Max's side.

Max had a few healing scrapes across his knuckles and a split lip that was fading, but other than that he looked unharmed. He had a bag in his hands, which he held out to Joss.

"Ohmigod," Joss moaned, ripping his seal skin out of the bag. He rubbed his face against it and held it tight to his chest like he was never going to let it out of his sight again. "Thank you, thank you, thank you."

Max gently lifted Danny and headed for the stairs. "You're welcome, kid. Do you need to go for a swim? I'm sure someone could take you to the harbor."

Danny pressed his aching head against Max's chest, his steady heartbeat soothing the tension in Danny's muscles.

"Maybe later. I just want to sleep for days right now. It's hard to be apart from it. It's like losing a piece of myself."

Max moved his hand so he could rest his palm against Danny's neck, and Danny whimpered in relief. The lights were still too bright, and the smell of the sandwiches on the sofa made his stomach lurch, but the pain that had speared through his head was manageable now.

"You should eat something before you go to sleep, Joss. You're too skinny. I'm going to make sure Danny gets some rest too."

Danny smiled against Max's shirt as Max carried him up the stairs, careful not to jostle him too much.

Max put him down in a cushy chair in the corner of the room that must have been his when he lived at home. Max's scent was stale, like he hadn't visited recently, but his was the most pervasive scent in the room.

He turned down the bed and moved like he was going to pick Danny up again, but Danny's dizziness had abated, and he wasn't going to let Max damsel him again. He stood up, shaky but okay, and made his way over to the waiting bed.

"Are you going to nap with me?"

Max worked open his belt. "After a shower, sure."

Danny watched him strip as he worked up the courage to ask how the raid had gone. He felt ridiculous, being afraid to bring it up, but he didn't know how he'd react if the witches had gotten away. Danny wasn't used to putting his life on the line like Max was—he didn't know if he could handle knowing that the people who wanted him dead were still out there.

"Did you get the coven?"

"The Enforcers did all the heavy lifting. Jackson and I were there to assist," Max answered. "They called in the Fae Guard to kill them since they could do it bloodlessly. Otherwise this case would have to be left open."

Danny was relieved they were dead, and he hated himself a bit for it.

"No more questions," Max said when Danny opened his mouth again. "You're going to nap till dinner. I'll wake you when it's time. Tori is bringing pancit just for you."

Danny's eyes were heavy, but he'd waited hours for Max, and he didn't want to go to sleep yet.

"Ray'd beat me up for it," he murmured.

Max chuckled. "He'd be on the floor as soon as he took the first step."

The promise of sibling violence made Danny smile. "Will you lie with me after you shower?"

Max tucked him in and kissed his neck. "Of course. I brought my paperwork here so I could work on it and watch over you. Officially Oscar and I got a tip and found the suspects dead in the warehouse. Jackson broke a gas pipe on the way out, so it will be attributed to that."

"Won't they run tox screens?"

Max snorted. "Listen to you. You consummate your mate bond with a cop and suddenly you're busting out words like tox screen? And no, it'll be fine. Alpha Connoll has a guy in the ME's office. Jackson's taking care of it."

Danny's eyes were heavy, and it was an effort to keep them open. But he wanted this time with Max, who was already heading to the bathroom.

"I'm sorry I didn't tell you I was trying to find Joss."

Max walked back and sat on the edge of the bed. He stroked Danny's hair. "I'm not going to say I'm not angry about that. But I get it now. Joss is family. I'd do the same for one of my nieces or nephews."

Max hadn't said *like* family. Danny forced his eyes open.

"Did you ask your parents to offer to foster Joss?"

Max's entire face lit up. "I didn't have to ask them. They saw a kid who needed help, and they acted on their own. Not that I wouldn't have asked them to—I just didn't need to."

Just when Danny thought he couldn't love this family more, something like this happened.

"Go take your shower so you can come back and cuddle me," he murmured.

Max left the T-shirt he stripped off on the bedside table, and Danny grabbed it without thinking, burying his nose in it as he curled up in bed. Knowing Max, it had probably been intentional. There rest of his clothes were in a heap by the bathroom door.

Danny's headache eased and his tension slid away. He fell asleep to the sound of the shower.

Chapter Fourteen

"**I'M** scarred for life," Sloane said as she draped herself dramatically on the blanket Max had set up in the shade.

He was shucking corn into a huge bowl to be cut up and added to the clambake they were having later this afternoon. One of Mrs. Cresswell's dearest friends, Ina, had offered her place in East Hampton for the Janus Foundation fundraiser, and it had spiraled and spiraled until it resembled nothing like the stuffy garden party she'd been planning.

Max couldn't be happier about that. He'd gotten more comfortable at stuffy formal fundraisers over the last few weeks, but he still appreciated the reprieve.

"Are you even listening? Aunt Veronica is wearing *shorts*, Max. I know you've only known her a month, but she doesn't wear shorts. I've never seen her wear shorts in my life. And she's elbow-deep in meringue, but she's *smiling*."

"I take it she's not much of a cook?"

"They're making a truckload of pavlovas. I've never even seen Aunt Veronica make a bowl of *cereal*, and she's in there making meringue with Ina."

"Give her a break. She's having fun. And she could hardly ask for a better teacher. Ina has the patience of a saint."

She'd insisted on making the food for the fundraiser. Max had been there when Mrs. Cresswell had mentioned a caterer—Ina had pitched a fit.

"It's bizarre. I can't believe she let you two talk her into turning afternoon tea into this. It's going to be a huge mess."

"I didn't have much to do with it. That was all Danny and Ina conspiring. But it was her own idea to invite the kids."

That had been a shock. Once they'd nixed the garden party, Mrs. Cresswell had decided to invite the foundation kids and their foster families. She'd rented buses to bring guests to the party.

Most of the foster families hadn't taken her up on it, but a few had. Joss was in charge of checking everyone into the bus and making sure they left on time. He'd matured so much since he'd come to live with Max's parents.

It had been three weeks since the witches had attacked them. Danny had taken a few days to recover from his concussion, and Joss had stepped up to help out at the foundation while Danny was stuck at home.

A shadow fell over the bushel, and a second later Danny dropped down onto the blanket. He smelled briny, and his skin was damp and clammy.

"Did you seriously go swimming?"

Danny grabbed an ear of corn and joined in the shucking.

"Just to cool off. I ran down from the marina."

Sloane's jaw dropped. "You ran down from Montauk?"

Danny grinned. "It's only, what, fifteen miles?"

She pointed a piece of corn at Max. "You broke him. I can't believe you ran fifteen miles like it's nothing."

"It is nothing," Danny said. "I mean, a month ago it probably would have killed me. But you'd be surprised how fast your body acclimates. Max and I started going for an evening run. It's actually pretty relaxing."

"Just wait until you've officially joined the Pack," Max said. "If you haven't been tuned in with the Connoll Pack, the power rush you're going to get from ours will be insane. Healthy Packs draw energy from each other."

Sloane frowned. "What if I don't want an energy boost?"

Max couldn't imagine *not* wanting to feel connected. "I don't mean energy boost like go run twenty miles energy. I mean, there will be some of that for you. More for Danny, since he's Alpha Mate. It's hard to explain. I guess it's more of a mental thing? Like, you know they like you, but now you can *feel* it."

"What if someone doesn't like you? Do you feel that?"

Max laughed. "A Pack bond isn't like a friendship. They can't dislike you on a Pack bond level. Like, take me. You annoy the ever-loving shit out of me most of the time, but my Pack bond to you is going to feel like nothing but love and acceptance. My brain might think you're a pain in the ass, but my heart knows you're Pack, and Pack is family."

Sloane threw a corncob at him, but she discreetly wiped her eyes after. He needed to remember that Sloane and Danny weren't coming from the best Pack situation. A lot of the better parts of Pack dynamics were lost on them because they'd never seen them in action.

"If that freaks you out, we can wait. You certainly don't have to join until you're ready, whether that's this moon or a moon six months from now or never. It's up to you."

"Are you thinking about not going through with it?" Danny asked, expression worried.

"No, I'm not backing out," Sloane said. "I'm joining with you."

Danny's grin was brighter than the late-morning sunshine. He tossed an ear of corn into the bowl. "What are we doing with these, anyway?"

"Ina said they were for the clambake," Max said. They'd made quick work of the bushel. He gathered up all the stalks and silk and pushed them into the basket. Ina had a huge compost pile on the back of her property, and he'd promised he'd dispose of them properly.

"You two take this up while I deal with these," he said. "I'm sure Ina and Mrs. Cresswell could use help in the kitchen."

"Wait, my mother is cooking?"

Max listened to Sloane moan about how traumatizing it was to see Danny's mother in the kitchen as they walked back up to the house. He composted the corn stalks and left the empty bushel basket by one of the dozens of raised garden beds. He'd been tasked with harvesting tomatoes for a salad later, and he'd grab it then.

The yard was beautifully landscaped and carefully tended. He'd have to make sure the kids stayed out of the gardens when they got here. Ina was a nymph of some sort—Max hadn't figured out exactly what her heritage was and it wasn't polite to ask—so at least she wouldn't faint if a witchling set her kohlrabi on fire.

The rest of the guests might. Today would be interesting, and Danny would need help keeping all the kids on their best behavior. They were all still riding high on the joy from the gifts Danny had passed out last week, so odds were good they'd behave as best they could.

Next week was the full moon. It didn't pull on Max, but he was still aware of it. All Supes were. They all experienced a bit of waxing and waning of their powers as the moon cycled. Only the werewolves were tied to it directly, but everyone felt it.

Max found a spot behind a shed and sat in the grass. He closed his eyes and turned his face to the sun, enjoying the warmth of the summer afternoon. He turned his focus inward, trying to achieve balance between his shifter side and his humanity. He'd been running on instinct since he inherited the Alpha power, and he needed to be more mindful about connecting the two. A good Alpha didn't let his instincts get the best of him. Max was managing, but only barely. It was a constant struggle, like a war inside him.

He didn't resent his grandmother for passing on the Alpha spark to him and not his father or one of his aunts or uncles. He understood that it was better for the new Alpha to be young. It ensured stability for the Pack in the long term. Outside of an emergency or the untimely death of an Alpha, the successor was always two generations younger than the Alpha.

Max hadn't been ready. Lola was only eighty-two. She was still strong and healthy. But he understood why she'd wanted to pass the mantle on. She wanted to travel and be free from the Alpha responsibilities while she could still enjoy it.

He'd been drowning these last few months. He'd only just managed to get his head above water when Danny came along, plunging him right back under. Finding his Alpha Mate was a blessing, and Max could never regret it, but what little control and balance he'd gained had disappeared as the bond wreaked havoc with his instincts.

Max let his hands fall to the ground, his claws extending and spearing into the soil. He'd been so caught up in easing Danny into the bond and keeping him safe, so focused on solving his case, that he hadn't checked in with himself in weeks. Hadn't thought about how the bond was affecting *him*. About how it felt having his Alpha Mate properly at his side. What it would do to his meager control to have Danny inside his head, not just as a mate but as Pack.

He smelled Danny before he heard him. Max retracted his claws and scrambled to dash away the tears that had gathered while he'd been meditating. By the time Danny came around the corner of the shed, Max had unlocked his phone and flipped to one of the dozens of browser tabs he had open.

Danny plopped onto the ground next to him. "What are you doing back here?"

"Watching videos on the proper way to eat lobster," Max said, showing him the screen. He didn't want Danny to know he had doubts about Danny joining the Pack so soon. The last thing he wanted to do was scare him. He was so skittish about the Alpha Mate bond— Max didn't want to give him reason to run away.

"Max," Danny said, unamused.

He had watched that video a few weeks ago, when he'd been so nervous about the gala they never attended. Lobster had been on the menu that night, and Max had been tied up in knots about embarrassing Danny with his table manners.

"Ina said she puts lobsters in her clambake," Max said, thumbing the screen off. He tossed the phone into the grass.

"They're cut in half and easy to eat," Danny said. "What's going on? Is this about what Sloane said? She's not really that nervous about joining the Pack, you know. She's just being herself."

"It's nothing." Max stood up and held a hand out to Danny. Instead of letting Max pull him up, Danny tugged hard on their joined hands and Max fell into his lap with an *oof*.

"It's not nothing, and we're not going up to the house until we talk about it. Alpha Mate, remember? Whatever you're thinking about had you upset enough I could feel it all the way up there."

Max rolled off Danny and lay on the ground, his arm shielding his eyes from the sun.

"It's just Alpha stuff."

Danny lay next to him on his side. Max could see him looking down at him, his face impassive.

"Alpha stuff is literally what an Alpha Mate exists to deal with," he said flatly.

Max sat bolt upright. "Not when the Alpha Mate is the problem!"

Danny paled, and Max reached out to grab him as he scrambled up. They were both on their knees, an arm's length apart, with Max's hands on his shoulders. They probably looked ridiculous, covered in grass.

"I didn't mean that."

"Yes, you did. It's the first honest thing you've said since I came back here."

Max winced. The urge to shift washed over him, but he swallowed it down. This was exactly what he'd been worried about. Confrontations with Danny shouldn't cause his instincts to go off the rails like that.

"I love you," Max said evenly. "I love you more than I thought it was possible to love another person. I love you more than my family. More than my Pack."

Danny sat on his heels, and Max let go of him, reassured he wasn't going to run before Max could explain.

"And that stresses you out? I thought an Alpha Mate was supposed to like, share the burden. I thought loving me was supposed to be a good thing."

He was making an awful mess of this. Shit.

"It is. And you do. But we're still learning, and the bond is still forming, and coming so close on the heels of my Alpha transition—sometimes it's just too much."

Danny's face went blank. "Too much?"

"Not like that. I can handle it."

"I don't want to be something you *handle*," Danny spat out.

"That's not—Danny, loving you is the best feeling I've ever had, okay? But my instincts are going fucking crazy. I'm trying to give you room to figure out your role in the Pack, but I want to be all over you. I'm flashing my eyes at people who bump into you on the street. Last week Ray took a hot dog off your plate, and I stabbed him in the thigh with my claws! That's not normal!"

Danny had regained color in his cheeks, but the scent of his hurt lingered in the air.

"I figured that was just a brother thing."

"No, it was an Alpha who keeps losing his shit kind of thing," Max snapped. He shouldn't be taking his frustration out on Danny. Max took a breath before he spoke again. "It's okay. I'm working it out. I was back here meditating. Trying to get my head on right before hundreds of people fill up this yard and every single one of them wants a piece of you. That's going to be hard for me to handle. It's going to be even more intense after you join the Pack, and to be honest, I'm worried about how I'll react."

"To me being part of the Pack?"

"To anyone trying to touch you after I've claimed you as mine in that ceremony."

Danny still looked confused and hurt, so Max started talking. He let all his anxieties out, telling Danny about the times his control had slipped. He started with the way he'd reacted to Danny in the helicopter on their first trip to Montauk and took him through every incident he could remember, right on up to growling at Sloane when she'd come into their bedroom on the yacht this morning to wake them up.

Danny looked stricken by the time he was done. "I had no idea. Max, you've got to tell me these things. You've got to let me know when you need something."

"That's just it," Max said. "What I need in those moments isn't rational. I can't lock you away in a tower, Danny. You're going to get pushed on the street and yelled at on the subway. I can't lose my shit every time that happens."

He braced himself for a lecture on Alpha asshole tendencies, but it never came. When he looked up, Danny was staring at him with wide-eyed amusement.

"One, I'd like to see you *try* to lock me in a tower. I'd eviscerate you. And two, how do you think I feel every time you go to work? It drives my wolf crazy that I can't protect you from all the horrible things you see and all the people who want to hurt you. It's a two-way street, buddy."

"But—"

"But nothing." Danny stood up, and Max followed suit. "I'm going to let Sloane know that we're postponing the induction ceremony indefinitely. You're going to talk to Lola about control, and we're going to keep exploring all the ways this Alpha Mate bond connects us. That way you can ease into it and not worry about having the Pack bond form at the same time. And when you're ready, I'll join the Pack."

"I promised—"

"Sloane isn't in any hurry. Neither am I. So what if we're Torres Pack in name only for a few more months? No one in the Pack is going to question that we deserve to be there, and if anyone outside the Pack has anything to say about it, they can go fuck themselves."

Max was too stunned to protest. He'd never seen Danny so assertive. Logically he'd known Danny could hold his own—he was a court advocate for children. He had to be assertive and sure of himself. But he'd never witnessed it himself. It was kind of awe-inspiring.

Danny grinned like he'd read his mind. "I'm the Alpha Mate. No one else in the Pack can give you orders except me. *That's* my role. To know what you need. You take care of the Pack, and I take care of you."

Max blinked back unexpected tears. "And you're okay with waiting to join the Pack?"

Danny shrugged. "Max, I've lived my entire life on the outskirts of a Pack. I know you can't understand that, because your connection to your Pack is pretty much a sixth sense to you, but I don't have that. I've never had that. So I'm not going to be languishing without it for the month or six we have to wait for you to settle into your Alpha spark. Same for Sloane. We'll be okay. The Pack *won't* be okay if its Alpha goes off the rails. So it's an easy choice."

Relief slammed through Max, making him weak in the knees. He felt a hundred pounds lighter, like his worry had been a physical thing he'd carried on his back.

"I love you," he told Danny. "I love you so much. I'm so excited to share my Pack with you. But you're right. I need to wait."

Danny beamed at him. "Look at you," he teased. "You've been mated to a therapist for almost a month and here you are, using words and expressing your emotions."

"Like a real adult."

"Speaking of adults, Alpha Connoll told us he wants Joss to wait until he's eighteen to join his Pack. It's not a bad idea. Joss has just started therapy, and I know he thinks he wants to join the Connoll Pack, but that could change."

Max had been a little offended when Joss announced he wanted to join the Connoll Pack, but after he'd had a little time to think about it, it made sense. Alpha Connoll had several selkies in his Pack, and it would be easier for them to mentor Joss if they were in the same Pack.

"His petition to adopt Joss was uncontested, so Joss will be a Connoll. He'll just be an informal Pack member for now."

Max was glad Joss had found a place in Connoll's family. He knew his parents wanted to adopt Joss as well, but Connoll was a better fit for him. Max's parents could love him, but they couldn't give him the kind of support Alpha Connoll could. The Torres Pack was big, but the Connoll Pack was massive. He had access to a lot of resources that Max and his family didn't. And Joss got along really well with Connoll's youngest son, Ryan. They were two peas in a pod, and it had done wonders for Joss to have someone close to his own age to hang out with.

Max took the hand Danny held out for him and let Danny pull him up.

"Ina wants me to make about twenty gallons of lemonade," he told Max. He batted his eyelashes. "She only has one citrus juicer, but I bet an Alpha would be able to do it with his bare hands."

"YOU might get hungry later," Ina said, pressing a box full of Tupperware containers into Max's hands.

He didn't see how that was possible. Her clambake fed two hundred, and no one went hungry. Max had eaten his fill and then some. Ina rented dozens of picnic tables and covered them all in huge sheets of parchment, and the easy atmosphere meant Max didn't have to worry about eating his lobster the right way. Danny, Sloane, and Ina had all circulated, helping the Janus Foundation kids who'd never seen a clambake before. It hadn't been like any of the fundraisers Max had attended with the Cresswells.

For starters, everyone had been wearing tacky plastic bibs with lobsters on them—and they'd loved it. Mrs. Cresswell hired a band, and the entire afternoon had been full of food, music, and yard games. The kids loved it, and so did Max.

"I don't know if we have room for all this on the boat," Max said, eyeing the box.

Ina waved off his concern. "Three shifters, two Weres, and a teenage selkie? You'll eat it before you go to bed tonight."

That was probably true. Ray and Tori were coming to spend the night, and Max and Danny were taking Joss out for a weekend sail after they left in the morning. Well, the captain was taking the boat for a sail. Max knew nothing about sailing, but the Cresswells' yacht had a full crew.

"There's an extra serving of pavlova in there too," Ina said with a wink. "Something for you and Danny to nibble on as a midnight snack. I remember how insatiable new mates are. Did you know my husband is a werewolf? Back when we bonded, J—"

Max bent down and kissed her on the cheek to cut her off. He liked her husband, and he wanted to continue to be able to look him in the eye.

"Thank you for everything, Ina. Next time you're in the city, you should come by. The Torres family lumpia recipe is the best you'll ever taste. We'd love to have you."

Ina clapped her hands together. "That sounds fantastic."

Sloane shouted for him from the car, and Max apologized as he rushed out the door. Tori raised an eyebrow when she saw the box but obligingly took it and rested it on her knees while he climbed in.

"Finally," Sloane said as Ray started the SUV. "I adore Ina, but she's a talker."

"She's lovely," Tori said. "And the food was amazing."

"It always is," Danny said from the passenger seat where he was squeezed in with Joss. "Remember the time we spent Thanksgiving there, Sloane?"

"Everything had at least two sticks of butter in it and tasted like angel tears and unicorns," she said dreamily. She turned to Max and rolled her eyes. "She can't stand Uncle Daniel, otherwise we'd go there every year. He was away for some big real estate deal that year."

"You'll spend it with us this year," Max said without thinking. "I mean—you can. You can spend it with us this year if you want to. Or not. If you don't want to. Because I would never Alpha order anyone to do anything. Especially in that case."

The car was silent, and he could have kicked himself for his misstep. They'd literally *just* talked about this, and he'd promised not let his Alpha get the best of him. And here he was, an Alpha asshole telling his mate he couldn't go home for Thanksgiving if he wanted to. Jesus.

Danny cracked up first, and everyone else followed suit. Max snapped his mouth shut and glared at his sister as she laughed until tears ran down her face.

"Ohmigod, your *face*," she gasped out.

Sloane elbowed him in the ribs. "I'd spend Thanksgiving with a roomful of strangers if it got me out of the formal dinner from hell Aunt Veronica usually has catered for us. Uncle Daniel insisted we spend it with them, but after tomorrow he's not going to have any say over what we do."

Danny turned around. "Uh, about that. I talked to Max and asked if we could move that back. It's too much change, too quickly. But obviously we won't be spending Thanksgiving in Manhattan, whether or not we're officially Pack by then."

Max appreciated Danny making up an excuse, but he didn't want to be the kind of Alpha who kept secrets.

"That's part of it, but I also wanted to wait because I'm not sure how my Alpha spark will handle it. I need some time to get that under control before we do it."

Sloane smiled. "It doesn't matter to me when we do it. I'm down, but I'm not in a rush."

The last bit of worry over postponing the ceremony evaporated, and Max breathed a sigh of relief. He'd been afraid Sloane would see it as a rejection, which couldn't be further from the truth. He wanted to be the best Alpha he could be for them, and unfortunately he wasn't living his best life at the moment, as his niece Jessica liked to say.

Tori reached across Sloane and squeezed his hand, and even Ray read the moment well enough that he didn't tease Max. They were closest to Max in age, and there was a reason they were the siblings he was closest to. If his cousin Bert resigned as Second, the two of them were his top contenders as a replacement. He'd been dreading the decision, but now he had someone to share that load with. As Alpha Mate, Danny would get a vote too.

He didn't have to do things alone anymore, and it was a huge relief. He had his family, his Pack, and his mate. Life was good.

Epilogue

Three Years Later

"YOU'RE sure you want to do this? You don't need more time? Severing from a Pack is a big decision. It can be undone, but your connection to the Pack will never feel the same," Max said as he knelt in the center of the circle his Pack had formed around them.

He was whispering, which Danny figured was more for the illusion of privacy than the actual thing. Everyone could hear, though they all kept their eyes on the ground in deference to their Alpha.

Danny held his breath. This was a big night for him. He was happy—God, he'd never been this happy—but a piece of him felt incomplete. He hadn't realized how much until now, when he was on the cusp of having everything he'd ever wanted.

"As the moon is my solemn witness," Veronica Cresswell said, "I petition to sever my ties with the Connoll Pack and join the Torres Pack as a full member. I pledge myself to your service, Alpha Torres, and to the service of your Pack."

Danny blinked back tears as he watched his mate flick a single claw out. Max slit a thin cut into his palm, then repeated the process with Danny's mother, who had held her hand out after her vow.

Max and Danny's two-year-old, Aidan, was perched on her hip. He had his fat little fingers tangled up in the pearls around her neck, a delighted expression on his face as he played with them.

"Veronica Cresswell, I welcome you into my Pack. I am honored to have you by my side. May the light of the Torres Pack embrace you. Your Pack sisters and brothers greet you."

The entire Pack spoke as one. "We pledge ourselves to you, sister. May our bond be blessed and fruitful."

Max held their palms together. "Veronica, do you promise to be a faithful member of the Torres Pack?"

"I do."

"Do you relinquish all other Pack bonds, both those you consented to and those that were forced upon you?"

They'd worked on the wording of this for weeks. His parents had divorced last year, just before Danny and Max had adopted Aidan. She'd still been bound to Danny's father with their mate bond, which he refused to sever. Alpha Connoll helped Max and Danny land on a vow that would cut all of his mother's ties, both to the Connoll Pack and to anyone else.

"I do so relinquish any previous bonds," his mother said.

Danny was proud of the way her voice didn't waver. She stood as straight-backed and confident as ever, but now that they were closer, Danny could see through the mask. She'd been as much a victim of his father's abuse as he was, and he was sorry it had taken thirtysome years for him to figure that out.

Max had jokingly asked if the Janus Foundation was a family business when they'd met, but now it was. His mother was their head of fundraising, and Joss, who was practically family even though he was officially a Connoll now, was juggling college and his job as activities director for the foundation.

Danny loved every minute of it. Especially because having more help at the foundation meant he could be home with Aidan more often.

Max put his free hand on Veronica's head. "As Alpha of the Torres Pack, I accept you into our bond. May the moon guide you and keep you, and may your bond forever serve as a reminder that you do not walk in this world alone."

Heat speared through Danny's chest. His eyes fluttered shut as he felt the bond he shared with Max flare open. Energy poured into him, and Danny had to fight to stay upright. He focused on holding on to the energy until a tug on the bond sent it flowing backward, into Max and out into the Pack.

They'd done a few rituals and blessings as a Pack since he'd taken his place as the Alpha Mate, but they hadn't inducted anyone. Danny hadn't been prepared for how strong the surge of power would be. As Alpha Mate he was a conduit for Max's Alpha power—a place for it to cycle through when it was too much for him.

It was always exhilarating, but tonight it set his hair on end. He felt alive and joyful and like he could run all night without stopping. He felt strong. Whole.

Max enveloped their newest member in a tight hug as soon as the ritual was finished. Danny hurried over and piled on, laughing when Aidan nestled his little face against Danny's neck and snuffled sleepily. He was a werewolf, so he couldn't feel the Pack bonds. Not yet at least. He was Pack, but until he Turned at nineteen, he was human.

That was a blessing tonight. All the other kids were wired, high on the Pack blessing and the energy surge. Oscar had come to stay with Aidan while the rest of the Pack ran for the full moon, as he had every moon since Max and Danny had agreed to foster Aidan.

"Someone's sleepy," Danny said, taking his son from his mother's arms. He carefully untangled his fat little fingers from the strand of pearls around his mother's neck. "I'd better get him put down so the run can start."

His mother kissed Aidan's cheek, and he stirred, opening one eye to look at her. "Gigi loves you, sweetheart. Sleep well."

Danny gave her a one-armed hug. "I'm glad you're here, Mother."

She looked so much younger when she smiled. "It's where I'm meant to be. Family should be Pack."

"And Pack should be a family," Max said as he walked up. He gave Danny a kiss and nuzzled against the top of Aidan's head.

"I'm going in," Danny said. He readjusted Aidan's dead weight in his arms and went inside.

His mother had helped them buy this house on the outskirts of Bear Mountain State Park two years ago as a wedding present. They had three acres that backed right up to the forest, giving them easy access for Pack runs. They'd taken to spending every full moon up here. Danny and Sloane might be part of a shifter Pack, but they still had Were urges. A good number of the Pack joined them each month.

Oscar was waiting for them in the living room. He held his hands out as soon as Danny came in, and Danny reluctantly transferred Aidan over. He'd been skittish when they'd first met him, but over the last year he'd gotten used to being transferred from person to person. The only time anyone put him down was to sleep in his crib. He was beyond spoiled, and after the rough start he'd gotten in life, he absolutely deserved every bit of indulgence they heaped on him.

"Everything go okay?" Oscar asked, his voice hushed.

"Perfect. We're heading out for the run now."

"Tori and I will have breakfast ready when you get back."

Oscar had taken his partner's secret identity as an Alpha shifter in stride. He and Sloane had dated on and off, but they'd been on now for over a year, and Danny was expecting a proposal any day now. Oscar would be formally brought into the Pack then in a ceremony similar to the one they'd had tonight. No blood would be spilled in deference to Oscar's inability to heal like a Supe, but the vows would be the same. He wouldn't be able to feel the Pack bonds, but the Pack would.

"Thanks." Danny gave Aidan one last kiss. "We won't have our phones on us, but if you need us—"

"Tori will be able to let you know through her mystical bond with you and Max, I know," Oscar said.

Danny went over this with him every month, but he couldn't help it. The first full moon after Aidan had come to them, he'd been so anxious he hadn't been able to leave the property. He'd run the perimeter, always close enough to hear Aidan's heartbeat. After that Max had started a rotation of Pack members who would stay at the house with Oscar, just in case.

"You're the best," he said over his shoulder as he let himself back out onto the porch.

Most of the Pack had already started sprinting, but Danny could sense Max lurking at the treeline. Danny undressed and shifted, loping off to meet his mate.

His heart soared when Sloane howled deeper in the forest, answered by a joyous howl from his mother and a chorus of higher-pitched howls from the rest of the Pack. Danny tipped his head up and joined in.

Three years ago Max had come to investigate a burglary and ended up stealing something much more valuable than the gifts in Danny's closet. He'd stolen Danny's heart, and when he'd given it back, it had been fuller than Danny ever imagined possible.

Now Available

Dreamspun Beyond #7
Camp H.O.W.L. by Bru Baker

Moonmates exist, but getting together is going to be a beast....

When Adrian Rothschild skipped his "werewolf puberty," he assumed he was, somehow, human. But he was wrong, and he's about to go through his Turn with a country between him and his Pack—scared, alone, and eight years late.

Dr. Tate Lewis's werewolf supremacist father made his Turn miserable, and now Tate works for Camp H.O.W.L. to ease the transition for young werewolves. He isn't expecting to offer guidance to a grown man—or find his moonmate in Adrian. Tate doesn't even believe in the legendary bond; after all, his polygamist father claimed five. But it's clear Adrian needs him, and if Tate can let his guard down, he might discover he needs Adrian too.

A moonmate is a wolf's missing piece, and Tate is missing a lot of pieces. But is Adrian up to the challenge?

Dreamspun Beyond #22
Under a Blue Moon by Bru Baker

Once in a blue moon, opposites find they're a perfect match.

Nick Perry is tired of helping people with their marriages, so when a spot opens up to work with teens at Camp H.O.W.L., he jumps at it. He doesn't expect to fall in lust with the dreamy new camp doctor, Drew Welch. But Drew is human, and Nick has seen secrets ruin too many relationships to think that a human/werewolf romance can go anywhere.

Happy-go-lucky Drew may not sprout claws, but he's been part of the Were community all his life. He has no trouble fitting in at the camp—except for Nick's stubborn refusal to acknowledge the growing attraction between them, and his ridiculous stance on dating humans. Fate intervenes when one of Drew's private practice patients threatens his life. Will the close call help Nick to see a connection like theirs isn't something to let go of?

Love Always Finds a Way

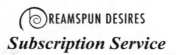

31901064760905